The Shakespeare Plot

Book 1

Assassin's Code

Alex Woolf

First published in Great Britain by Scribo MMXVII
Scribo, a division of Book House, an imprint of
The Salariya Book Company
25 Marlborough Place, Brighton, BN1 1UB
www.salariya.com

ISBN 978-1-911242-38-3

Book Design by David Salariya

Printed and bound in China

The text for this book is set in Cochin
The display type is P22 Operina

www.salariya.com

Artwork Credits
Front cover illustration: Andrea Da Rold
Fron[illegible] Hans Holbein the Younger
Gatef[illegible] Collection / Look and Learn
[illegible]

The Shakespeare Plot

Book 1

Assassin's Code

Alex Woolf

Prologue

31st January 1601

A freezing wind blew in from the river. Richard Fletcher pulled his woollen cloak closer around his neck to keep out the cold. He could hear the echoing roar of the Thames as it rushed beneath the supports of London Bridge. Glancing to his left, he saw the heads of five traitors stuck on spikes above the bridge's gateway.

He shivered at the gruesome sight and hurried on, leaving the bridge and river behind him and plunging into a twisting maze of narrower lanes. The buildings on either side seemed to press in on him. Their upper stories jutted out so far over the street that it was often hard to see the sky. And running between them were dark and scary alleyways that echoed with drunken shouts, barking dogs and screaming infants.

In his left hand, Richard gripped a ragged paper scroll.

'Deliver this message!' the fellow had snarled at him that morning. *'If you don't, I will expose your sister's secret!'*

No one could ever know about Alice's secret. It would mean the end of everything...

A sudden clatter of horse's hooves on cobbles and a screech of wheels made Richard bolt to the side of the road. He took refuge in the shadow of a building as a cart hurtled by.

'Gardy-loo!' a woman cried out. Richard stepped to one side just as a bucketful of urine was poured from a window directly above him. It splashed into the gutter where he'd been standing, and some of it splattered his cloak.

'I want to be gone from here,' he muttered to himself, and he wished more than ever that he was back home at his lodgings on the south side of the river – back with Alice.

But first he would have to make this delivery. He had no choice. If the truth ever got out about Alice, she would be ejected from their company of players, the Chamberlain's Men. Richard would have to go, too – he could never desert his sister. They would be forced out of the only place they had ever felt loved or cared for. Where would they go instead? Back to that terrible orphanage where they grew up? Never! Richard could imagine no other life for himself but being a player at the Globe.

'Deliver the message to Mr Jasper Scrope, who lives above the Bell Savage Inn. Make sure to hand it to him personally.'

Those were the instructions he'd been given.

The inn, so he'd been told, lay on the western edge of the city, near the Lud Gate. The trouble was, in this labyrinth of narrow, winding streets, Richard could no longer be sure that he was even heading west. And to make matters worse, the light was now dimming in the sky. The shopkeepers were putting up their shutters, and the vendors were packing away their stalls. Soon, the streets would belong to thieves, murderers and cutpurses.

As Richard continued his cautious progress, a surly-looking gang of apprentices in leather doublets and woollen caps appeared out of the gloom, jostling him as they passed. One stared at him with a nasty gleam in his eye. Richard wished he'd brought along his dagger.

This was a fool's errand he was on! What could be of such importance in this tattered scroll that he was obliged to endanger life and limb to deliver it? Before setting out, Richard had taken a peek at the words and symbols written on the paper, and had been mystified by them. He'd taught himself to read soon after joining the Chamberlain's Men as a prentice. It was a necessary skill for any aspiring player. Yet the words in this message were not in English – nor did they look pronounceable by any human tongue. He could only conclude that they had been written in some sort of secret code. But what kind of message needed to be written in code? And why not entrust its delivery to an ordinary courier?

The more he thought about it the more convinced he became that this was some sort of criminal business he had become embroiled in. This scared him, but also made him curious. He'd even written out a copy of the message, which he'd left in a chest under his bed, intending to take another look at it on his return. Perhaps, in time, he would be able to divine its meaning.

The street he was walking down finally ended in a cobbled yard. In the middle was a public stocks, surrounded by decaying fruit and vegetables that had recently been hurled at offenders imprisoned there. On the far side stood a large gate set into a three-storey building – part of London's wall. Richard was relieved to see that he had reached the edge of the city. It was almost fully dark by now, and he spied a watchman out on patrol, carrying a pikestaff and a bell. Richard approached him. 'Sir, can you tell me where I am?'

'The Lud Gate,' said the heavily bearded man, indicating the gate.

'And where can I find the Bell Savage Inn?'

The watchman looked Richard up and down.

'Are you sure you want that establishment, young man? 'Tis the haunt of rogues and conmen.'

'Prithee sir, just tell me which way to go!' pleaded Richard.

The man pointed along a shadowy lane. Richard thanked him and began walking down it, heart thumping in his chest. Several times he nearly slipped on the slimy cobbles, filthy with the waste from butcher shops and open sewers. Once, he had to pull up sharply to avoid falling into a cartwheel rut filled with fetid water. Scrawny, barefoot children ran past him like pale ghosts. Beggars, both male and female, lurked in doorways, holding out their thin hands as he went by. He knew that desperation – he and Alice had been forced to beg during a terrible winter two years ago, after their escape from the orphanage and before they had found a new life at the Globe. One beggar had no legs. He rested his stumps on a small wooden platform on wheels. Pushing himself along on this rickety construction, he trailed after Richard.

'Alms for a poor wounded soldier, served queen and country in Ireland,' he croaked.

Richard couldn't look the man in the eye as he pressed a penny into his palm.

Further along, he passed a boarded-up house with a red cross painted on the door, and beneath it the words: Lord have mercy upon us. With a shudder, he realised it was a plague house.

Finally, Richard reached the inn. A sign directed him through a low-ceilinged tunnel into a courtyard. The cobbles here were almost obscured beneath a carpet of sawdust and discarded hazelnut shells. The place smelled of dry blood and stale beer. Richard caught sight of a bear skull in the sawdust. They must stage animal fights here, he guessed. He pushed open a heavy wooden door and entered the inn. The heat and noise of the place were a shock to the senses. There were men seated around tables, drinking flagons of ale and singing. Others were engaged in rowdy games of dice. Their faces were hard, their eyes cold. The jollity had a dangerous edge. Richard approached a maid carrying a tray of meat pies.

'Excuse me!' he shouted above the raucous singing, 'I'm looking for a Mr Jasper Scrope.'

She looked at him with startled eyes. 'Are you sure you want *him,* sir?'

Richard nodded.

She was about to reply when a volley of angry shouts exploded from one of the dice-playing tables.

'Why, you toad-spotted malt-worm!' roared a big, red-faced man. 'You gleeking, flap-mouthed puttock! These dice are loaded!'

'How dare you, you beslubbering, swag-bellied boar-pig!' cried the one he'd accused. 'Take back your words or feel the sharp edge of *this*!' He drew his rapier.

The big man thundered more colourful curses and charged at his adversary, who fell backwards under his weight, clattering into a table and spilling tankards of foaming beer. This raised more furious voices and, out of nowhere, a full-scale brawl erupted. Richard backed into a corner as wild punches and kicks were thrown, and stools and tankards were hurled across the room. Someone spilled the maid's tray, and she fell to her knees, scrambling around to pick up the fallen pies.

'You'll find him up there, the door at the end!' she shouted at Richard, pointing through an arched exit at the back of the room that led to a twisting set of steps. Richard ducked as a man swung a heavy iron poker, missing his head by inches, and raced towards the stairway. At the top of the steps, he paused, leaned against a wall and wiped his brow. From below came the muffled sounds of the fight. *See this thing through, then get out of here as fast as you can,* he told himself.

He was at one end of a crooked corridor of dark oak beams. The floorboards creaked as he walked along the passage. When he came to the last of the doors, he took a deep breath and knocked. There was no reply, so he knocked again.

'Mr Scrope?' he called. He heard a faint scuffling from within. 'Mr Scrope? Is that you?'

'Who wants me?' came a low, sighing voice that filled Richard with inexplicable dread. Somehow he managed to reply: 'My name is Richard Fletcher. I'm a prentice with the Chamberlain's Men, at the Globe playhouse. I was sent here to deliver you a message.'

'Who was it sent you?'

Richard told him.

He heard some footsteps, a latch was raised and the door creaked open. The room within was dark, save for some embers glowing in the hearth and a faint glow of moonlight from a balcony at the back. The figure standing before him was completely covered by a hooded cloak. Richard couldn't see the man's face, yet he knew he was being scrutinized by a pair of eyes set deep within the shadow of that hood.

'Enter,' whispered the man. His breathing sounded strained and clogged with phlegm, and Richard wondered if he was suffering from some disease of the lungs.

As he entered the room, Richard heard the door swing closed behind him. He had the horrid feeling he'd been lured into a trap. His hand shook as he handed the scroll to the man. Bony fingers reached out from the cloak and snatched it from him, and the figure moved back to the fireplace. Scrope touched a taper to a glowing coal and lit a candle, which he held close to the scroll, now unfurled. For a long time, he studied the paper.

He can read the code, thought Richard. Again, he wondered what it said. He would work that out later. Right now, his only desire was to get away from this odious place and put the whole, frightening episode behind him.

'If that is all,' he said to the hooded figure, 'I shall take my leave.' He began backing towards the door.

'Stay!' croaked the man.

Richard froze.

'Do not move from where you are!'

What does he want with me? fretted Richard. *I've done my part – I've delivered the message…*

In the candlelight, Scrope's figure cast a huge, juddering shadow across the wall and ceiling of the room. 'Did you read this?' he wheezed, brandishing the scroll at him.

'No,' said Richard.

'Good!'

The man touched the candle flame to the rag-paper, which smouldered and then caught fire. He flung it into the hearth. Whatever message it had contained must have been too dangerous to be allowed to exist – even in coded form.

Richard watched the scroll curl and blacken into ash. He was too absorbed to notice, and then too slow to react, as the man drew a sword from his belt, rushed forwards and swung it hard towards his head.

He felt a sudden, horrid crack in his skull, then everything went dark.

Act One

1st ~ 2nd February 1601

Chapter 1

Alice's Secret

Alice Fletcher stirred as the grey dawn light seeped through the casement above her bed and lit her eyelids. She blinked a few times – then relaxed. It was Sunday, her day off! She could sleep a little longer today, and still be up in time for church. After a few minutes, remembering something, she twisted round to peer across the room towards her brother's bed. She was surprised to see it empty. Richard must have risen already – it was very unlike him to wake so early on a Sunday.

How disappointing! She'd been looking forward to asking him where he'd gone to yesterday. He'd been so furtive all morning, not saying a word to her, and then as soon as Mr Armin had dismissed them from rehearsals in the afternoon, he just took off without even saying goodbye. Usually he invited her along if he was going on one of his hunting trips into the countryside. It was all so mysterious!

She would have waited up for him last night, but she'd been so tired after a hard week working on the visual and sound effects at the Globe. How irritating of him to disappear like this! But as she began to think more deeply about the matter, she felt a tingle of something much worse than disappointment – fear. Richard's bedclothes weren't crumpled – they were perfectly flat and smooth. He obviously hadn't slept here last night. So where was he?

Alice climbed out of bed. As usual, she got dressed in a linen tunic, woollen stockings and a sheepskin doublet. She'd been dressing as a boy for so long, it no longer seemed strange. She did it because she had to. The theatre, where she and Richard worked, was a male-only world. Women and girls weren't allowed to act on the stage, and female parts were always played by boys. So Alice had turned herself into Adam. She cut her hair short, wound a cloth tightly around her chest and wore boy's clothing. She was Adam at the playhouse, Adam at home, Adam at the market and everywhere else she went. She had agreed with Richard that it was safest that way. No one would be allowed to know the truth, not even Edmund Squires, her closest friend at the Globe. Alice had played the part for so long, she sometimes almost forgot that she was a girl at all. And for two years the deception had worked. No one knew her secret. She and Richard were safe.

Once she was dressed, Alice ran downstairs, hoping against hope to find her brother in the kitchen eating his breakfast.

He wasn't there.

Instead, she found Mrs Fairfax, their landlady, making acorn bread.

'Good morrow, young sir,' beamed Mrs Fairfax.

'Good morrow, mistress,' replied Alice. 'Have you seen my brother Richard?'

Mrs Fairfax frowned in thought. 'Not since yesterday as I recall.'

Alice slumped onto a bench by the hearth and warmed herself there. 'I don't know what's become of him.'

'Ah, he'll return soon enough,' said Mrs Fairfax as she kneaded the stiff dough with her chubby, flour-dusted hands. 'The smell of my fresh-baked bread will tempt him back if nothing else. Young men are ruled by their stomachs, as you must know.'

'Where do you suppose he's gone?'

'I dare say he went carousing with his friends, and now he's sleeping it off in a tavern in the Paris Garden or some other unseemly part of Southwark.'

'I do hope you're right,' said Alice, though she was pretty sure her brother was not the carousing type.

'You're a good lad, Adam,' said Mrs Fairfax, 'but many young men of your age are possessed of a more wayward spirit. You cannot tame them. I could never tame my George. It took the army to do that.' She sniffed. 'He's never been the same since he came back from Ireland.'

Mrs Fairfax often talked of her son's terrible experiences over in Ireland fighting under the Earl of Essex against the rebels. On the few occasions George had visited, he'd never uttered a word to anyone. Mrs Fairfax would fuss over him like a mother hen, but he would scarcely react, and his eyes seemed empty of all feeling.

'Would you like something to eat, Adam? I have smoked herring, and eggs fresh laid this morning.'

'Maybe later, mistress. Thank you,' said Alice, and she drifted out of the kitchen and back upstairs to their chamber. Perhaps she could find some clue to her brother's whereabouts among his possessions. She pulled out his personal chest from under his bed, located the key in the usual hiding place inside his copy of the Bible, and opened it.

In there, she found Richard's spare tunic and a few other items of clothing, along with his dagger and his pewter bowl and cup. There was no sign of his most treasured possession, though – the locket on a chain. It puzzled Alice to find this missing, as Richard had sworn never to wear it but to always keep it here safely in his chest. The locket was the only connection they had with their mother. She had left it, along with the two of them, on the steps of the orphanage thirteen years ago, when they were little more than babes. Inside the beautifully engraved silver case was a miniature portrait of a woman who they had to assume was their mother.

A priest – one of the few kindly souls in that cold and brutal orphanage – had given the locket to Richard when he turned ten. Receiving the locket and being able to gaze upon their mother's face for the first time had filled both children with joy, but also awoke in them a burning question: why had this beautiful lady abandoned them? The priest, sadly, had no answer to this. All he could say was that, whatever her reasons, it would not have been because she did not love them.

Richard had accepted this and was comforted by it. A year older than Alice, he claimed to remember their mother singing to him as he lay in her arms. He believed that some twist of fate outside of her control had forced her to give them up. Alice had agreed with him at first, but as she grew older, her opinion changed. She grew to despise her mother for abandoning them, and blamed her for every torment and humiliation they suffered at the orphanage. Alice sometimes wished she'd never set eyes on the locket, and it troubled her to note how much she had begun to resemble the face inside it.

But now the locket was gone. So Richard must have taken it with him. What could have induced him to take such a risk? She was so busy pondering this mystery that she almost failed to spot something else in the chest – something quite unexpected. When her eye, at length, fell upon it, peeping out from beneath a fold of cloth, she gave a start.

A scroll.

What could this be? Had Richard taken home his *role*? The role was a sheet of paper containing a particular player's part in a play, together with his cues – the lines just before his speeches. Perhaps Richard had needed more time to memorize his part in their forthcoming production of the latest play by Will Shakespeare, the company's playwright.

The play was about a Danish prince called Hamlet, and Richard had been given a very important part. He was due to play Ophelia, the girl Hamlet was in love with. He'd confessed to Alice that he was apprehensive about the part. Even so, he must have known there was a strict ban on removing roles from the playhouse premises, due to the danger of theft. Such was the demand for new plays in London that unscrupulous companies often stole plays from their rivals. That was why the only complete copy of each play was kept under lock and key in the props room at the Globe, and the players were forbidden from taking their roles home with them.

Nervously, Alice unfurled the scroll. But instead of finding Ophelia's lines there, she was confronted by what looked like complete nonsense. It was just a long string of random-looking characters without any spaces between them…

goefburrcadiilegethsvrsihiewbetrlaeldtsiekldlvrrfhsesglb7erayihriklbalateeodwtnnonrabeesaluyrtsileieeotinsae

Beneath this gibberish were two scribbled drawings. One of these showed a horse and carriage with a zig-zag line alongside it. The other one looked like a coat of arms. It showed the head of a leopard over a fleur de lys.

What is this? thought Alice. She studied it intently for several minutes, and the more she studied it the more certain she became.

'It's a secret code,' she whispered to herself. The characters and symbols meant something, though she'd need to know the code's key if she was to decipher it. But why did Richard have a coded message in his chest? She wracked her memory, trying to recall anything he'd said over the past few days that might connect to this. He'd certainly been nervous recently, but she'd assumed that was because of his forthcoming performance as Ophelia. Had there been something else on his mind? He normally told her everything, or she assumed he did. After all, she'd always confided in him.

Yet she had to accept that things had changed lately.

She had grown closer to other people at the Globe, especially Edmund Squires, one of the prentices, and Richard had begun to make friends with some of the hired men and the sharers – the senior members of the company. Perhaps he'd found others to share his innermost thoughts and feelings with. The thought saddened her.

Then she recalled an incident a few days ago. She had been in the Globe's central yard, sweeping up the mess left by the groundlings after an afternoon show, when she'd heard voices...

Glancing up, Alice saw Richard standing at the entrance of the Tiring-House, the room at the back of the stage where the players changed between scenes. He was deep in conversation with someone inside the room, though she couldn't see who. Following this exchange, Richard wandered out onto the stage looking pensive, even worried.

'What's wrong?' she called out him.

He looked up, startled to see her there, and forced a smile. 'As stars with trains of fire and dews of blood, Disasters in the sun…'

'*Hamlet,* right?' said Alice.

Richard nodded. Then he looked around furtively to make sure they weren't being overheard, and added: 'There are dangers here, Ali. Plots are being hatched. People aren't all they seem.'

'That doesn't sound like Shakespeare any more.'

'No, this is me talking,' said Richard.

She'd wanted to ask him more, but at that point Mr Armin had appeared and called Richard away for a rehearsal. Alice hadn't known what to make of Richard's words or his strange mood. But the next time she saw him, he'd seemed more cheerful and they'd spoken of other things. Now she wished she'd forced him to tell her more. What did he mean by 'People aren't all they seem', and 'Plots are being hatched,' and did it have anything to do with this coded message?

Chapter 2

The Earl of Essex

Tom Cavendish ducked just as the priceless Venetian glass goblet sailed inches over his head, smashing against the wall behind him. Pieces of shattered glass bounced on the polished stone floor. Tom's smart servant's livery was now spattered with droplets of wine. He tried to control his shaking, telling himself he ought to be used to this by now. His master, Robert Devereux, the Earl of Essex, was in one of his rages. The earl prowled the room, face like thunder, pounding his fist on any available surface and shouting: 'We'll destroy those vipers! We'll take back the kingdom!'

There was a broom by the hearth, kept there for this very purpose. Tom began sweeping up the mess of broken glass, trying to shut out the sound of his master's anguished bellows. Tom had been a servant at Essex House, the earl's London residence, for almost a year now, and it had rarely been a happy or peaceful place. The rages themselves never lasted long. What followed was in some ways worse: a prolonged bout of despair.

His fury now spent, the earl collapsed into a chair, put his bruised hands to his face and groaned. 'I was her favourite once, Tom. But her mind has been poisoned against me!'

Tom had been tutored on how to help the earl when he was in one of these moods. *Get him talking about the old times,* Sir Gelly Meyrick, the steward, advised. *Sometimes it works.*

So Tom asked him: 'What was it like, my lord, when you were the queen's favourite?'

The earl wiped his eyes and glanced at Tom, the beginnings of a smile dawning at the edges of his lips. 'She loved me,' he said. 'She loved me more deeply than anyone since Robert Dudley. I spoke to her like she was a woman, not just a monarch. I made her laugh. She showered me with titles. I was Master of the Horse, a member of the Privy Council. And I repaid her with stunning victories over her enemies. Did I ever tell you, Tom, how I captured the Spanish city of Cadiz, back in '96?'

'Nay, sir,' said Tom, though he had heard the story many times. He put aside his broom and listened once again. His excitement wasn't entirely feigned, for it was a thrilling story, and what was more, it seemed to grow more dramatic with each retelling. Today, the earl led just 500 men ashore, and they charged across the boiling sand and faced down a thousand Spanish cavalry. Last time, Tom was sure, the numbers had been the other way around.

'I was first through the city walls,' said the earl. 'Sword in hand, I hacked down all who stood in my way. With just a handful of men I pushed my way towards the centre of the town…'

He was on his feet, swinging an imaginary sword, attacking a Spaniard in the guise of an iron candle stand. The Earl of Essex was tall and strong, with a long nose, a broad, pale face and a square-cut beard. He looked every inch a warrior.

But his burst of exuberance did not last, for the memories he had conjured served only to highlight how far he had fallen. After killing a few more Spaniards, the earl cast aside his imaginary sword and stared miserably into the hearth.

'Back in England, jealous courtiers began campaigning for my downfall. They set a trap for me, sending me to Ireland to put down the rebellion there. The rebel forces were powerful, and I wasn't provided with adequate troops. All my requests for reinforcements were denied.'

Tom saw his master's jaw tremble as he stared into the guttering flames. He wished he could lead him away from these dark thoughts – away from Ireland, back to Spain – but he did not know how.

'We suffered ambush and disease in that treacherous, bog-filled land,' said Essex. 'And my critics at court, most of whom had never seen a battlefield in their lives, carped at me for concluding a truce with the rebel leader instead of crushing him as they had demanded… On my return to England, I was stripped of my titles and banished from court in disgrace.'

'Come, my lord,' said Tom, 'Pray be seated. Let me pour you some wine…'

The earl turned on him, eyes ablaze, as if Tom were somehow to blame for his misfortunes.

'I was forced to remain here in this house, like a common prisoner.' He kicked at the stone hearth. 'But those scheming ministers weren't finished with me. They wanted to make Essex poor as well as powerless. So they persuaded the queen to take away my most important source of income – the taxes I earned on the import of sweet wines from the east.'

Tom remembered that day well, for the earl had smashed enough crockery and glassware to feed a small banquet, and it had been Tom's job to sweep it all up.

'But they don't know the man they are dealing with, my lord!' roared a powerful, Welsh-accented voice from the far end of the hall.

Tom looked up to see Sir Gelly Meyrick striding into the room. The fiery steward had been one of the earl's fiercest and most loyal soldiers on his military campaigns, and was eventually knighted by Essex for his service. 'You will have your revenge on them one day, my lord!' he cried. 'And most especially on the worst of them, by which I mean, of course, the Beagle!'

The Beagle was the nickname they had bestowed on the queen's chief minister, Robert Cecil – the leading voice in the campaign against the Earl of Essex. Tom had often heard his name spoken in this house. It was always uttered in anger, and often preceded by phrases like 'that vile goblin' or 'that evil elf', but most often he was simply referred to as the Beagle.

Tom had never seen Cecil, but he guessed from these names that the man was small in stature. He imagined him as a tiny, wizened old man, constantly scheming against the earl and whispering lies about him into the queen's ear.

'Aye,' muttered the earl. 'I will have my revenge.'

From outside came the noise of men shouting. Another little band of warriors had arrived in the inner courtyard – the fourth such to arrive in the past hour. The courtyard had become the scene of a surprising amount of activity in recent days. Messengers from the earl's friends and allies were constantly arriving and departing. Rough-looking soldiers were mustering there, finding temporary quarters in the stable block or under canvas tents. Carts carrying barrels of provisions trundled across the cobbles, arriving at a rate of two or three an hour. It was as if Essex House were a castle preparing for a siege.

Tom wondered whether the planned revenge against Cecil – which Sir Gelly and the earl had been talking about for months now – was finally about to happen. Would the Beagle get his comeuppance? The idea was strangely exciting to Tom.

Yet he had little time to ponder these larger events, for now Sir Gelly sent him off on an errand, and he was kept busy the rest of the morning fetching wood, trimming candle wicks, keeping the room fires stoked and waiting on the earl's many guests. At around midday he was ordered to take wine to the earl in his private chambers.

Essex was sitting for a portrait when Tom entered. Despite his financial difficulties, the earl was dressed expensively, as was his habit, in the finest velvet doublet and a cambric ruff. He turned, and beamed. 'Ah, there's my boy Tom with the wine!'

Tom was relieved to find his master in better spirits.

The artist tutted. 'Prithee, my lord. I cannot paint if you will keep moving.'

'And I cannot drink if you will keep painting,' rebutted Essex cheerfully. 'Sirrah, be gone now. Return here tomorrow at the same hour.'

As the artist packed away his easel and departed, Tom poured his master his wine.

'You will have noted all the comings and goings these past few days, Tom,' said the earl.

'Aye, my lord,' said Tom.

'Well, be not troubled by it.'

'How so, my lord?'

'We are taking a few precautions, that is all.' Essex drank deeply from his goblet. 'My enemies may be planning a move against me, and we are preparing our defences.'

'Do they really mean to attack us?'

'I know not, but the signs are ominous. Some days ago, my good friend the Earl of Southampton was attacked in broad daylight by Lord Grey, one of Robert Cecil's creatures. It was a vicious, unprovoked assault, during which he actually chopped off the hand of Southampton's page.'

'That is awful, my lord.'

'It was a shot across the bows, Tom. Next time, they may decide to target me. As I said, we must be prepared…'

Just then, the door to the chamber opened and Sir Gelly came in, accompanied by Lord Monteagle, a friend of the earl's.

Sir Gelly seemed consumed with righteous fury. Predicting a storm, Tom retreated into the shadows.

'My lord, the Beagle has just sent us a warning,' declared Sir Gelly, brandishing a sheet of parchment. '"Her Majesty," he informs us, "is alarmed by the swaggering swordsmen fighting in your yard. She disapproves of the lavish entertainment you are offering to your noble friends and is concerned that you mean to establish a rival court at Essex House. She demands that you desist in these activities forthwith."'

Essex leapt to his feet, strode over to Sir Gelly

and snatched up the note. He stared at it for several moments, and Tom saw the spots of angry colour blooming in his pale cheeks. Then he crushed it in his fist and hurled it into the fire.

'How dare the Beagle presume to speak for the queen!' he snarled. 'I was her favourite when he was a nothing – a mere Member of Parliament. I know her, and I know she did not say any of this.'

'He is a miserable spider,' sneered Sir Gelly.

'A spider who unfortunately sits upon the queen's shoulder,' said Lord Monteagle.

'The queen is well aware that I cannot abide a life without music and dancing and swaggering sword fights,' said the Earl of Essex. 'If I am to be denied these pleasures at her court, then I must create them for myself here. We are warriors and pleasure-seekers, are we not, my friends? Our natural domains are the battlefield and the banqueting hall – places that are entirely foreign to the milk-livered, quill-pushing Robert Cecil!'

This speech elicited a 'Hear, hear!' and a pounding on the table from Sir Gelly.

'Fie upon him!' cried the earl. 'We shall make such a din here at Essex House that will be heard across the city from Whitehall Palace to the Tower of London, what say you gentlemen?'

'Hear, hear!' bawled Sir Gelly once more. 'We'll show the Beagle what we think of his cowardly threats.'

Monteagle's assessment was more sober. 'We should

redoúble our defences,' he said. 'This letter is only the beginning. My guess is that he's planning an assault.'

'I will place extra guards on the gate,' said Sir Gelly.

'It's not enough,' said Monteagle. 'We must seize the initiative before he has a chance to attack.'

Monteagle had a long face, solemn eyes and a well-groomed beard. He wore his family insignia – a leopard's head over a fleur de lys – prominently upon his chest. Yet his dignified appearance concealed a rebellious heart. He was a Roman Catholic – a dangerous thing to be in Protestant England – and he had been connected to several plots against Elizabeth over the years. Somehow, though, he had always managed to evade arrest. These days he was a supporter of Essex. Even though the earl was a Protestant, they had found common cause in their mutual hatred of the Beagle.

Monteagle fixed the earl with a baleful stare, and lowered his voice. 'I have a plan, Robert,' he said, 'that could solve all our problems at one fell swoop.'

The earl looked at him with sudden interest, but before he could question Monteagle further, a groom entered the chamber. 'My Lord,' he said, bowing to the earl, 'Sir Francis Bacon has arrived and wishes to speak with you.'

Chapter 3

Sir Francis Bacon

Tom, watching from a corner of the room, noticed a change in the earl's countenance as his frown was replaced by a hopeful smile. 'Francis!' he grinned. 'Now there's a man I can trust. Perhaps he has some news from court. Show him in.'

The groom bowed again and disappeared.

'Be careful, Robert,' Lord Monteagle warned the earl. 'This could be another of the Beagle's tricks. He knows how much you like Sir Francis. He may have persuaded him to talk to you.'

'Tush, sir!' cried Essex. 'Francis is his own man. Always has been.'

At that moment, Sir Francis swept into the room. He was a small man with sharp, curious eyes, reddish-brown hair and a neat, pointed beard. He embraced the much taller Essex and inclined his head politely towards the other men.

Tom had met Sir Francis on previous visits and had always liked him. Sir Gelly had once told him that Sir Francis was a philosopher as well as a courtier, and one of the cleverest men in England. Yet there was nothing vain about him. He spoke to everyone, whether they were an earl or a footman, in the same courteous and respectful tone. Perhaps it was because he was so universally liked that Sir Francis had been able to remain on good terms with both Essex and the court. This made him the ideal intermediary between the two camps.

'Robert,' he said, coming immediately to the point, 'you know I have been working strenuously these past few months to restore you to favour. I have been trying to persuade the queen to show clemency, particularly in the matter of the licence for sweet wines, and I am pleased to say I have been making some progress in that direction.'

'You have?' exclaimed the earl, overjoyed.

'Aye, Robert, I believe so. But my efforts are being severely undermined by all these strange goings-on at Essex House. Is that some sort of rag-tag army you are assembling in your courtyard?'

'What would you have me do, Francis?' said the earl with a frown. 'You know that Cecil means to crush me.'

'Cecil will do nothing without the approval of the queen,' Sir Francis assured him. 'Give me a few more days, Robert. Let me speak with her again. In the meantime, I urge you to stay calm and not do anything rash.'

'You will speak to her again?' cried Essex. 'Do you promise?' And he looked to Tom at that moment like a naughty child begging his nurse to plead with his mother to show mercy.

Sir Gelly's jaw tightened and Monteagle shook his head disapprovingly.

'It's too late for all that, Robert,' said Monteagle. 'There can be no going back, not while the Beagle holds sway at court.'

'You don't know that, William,' said Sir Francis sternly, addressing Monteagle by his given name. 'It is for the queen alone to make these decisions. Now, if you will excuse me gentlemen, I must get back to the palace.'

Essex gripped his arm. 'I shall wait upon your word, Francis.'

Sir Gelly told the groom, who had been waiting discreetly by the door, to fetch Sir Francis's hat and cloak. But Sir Francis shook his head and pointed at Tom. 'This boy can show me out,' he said.

Tom, who had thought himself unseen, gave a start of surprise. 'Aye, sir,' he said, scurrying across the room in time to open the door for the departing philosopher. He was grateful for the opportunity to spend a few moments in the company of the great

Sir Francis Bacon, yet at the same time he was also slightly regretful that he would miss hearing about Monteagle's plan to solve all of Essex's problems 'at one fell swoop'.

As Tom led Sir Francis along the corridor that would take them back to the main staircase, Sir Francis suddenly spoke: 'It's Tom, isn't it?' he asked.

'You remembered, sir!' said Tom with a flush of joy. They had only had one very brief conversation and that had been several weeks ago.

'I try to remember everyone I meet,' said Sir Francis, 'especially the ones who impress me... You didn't miss a word of that conversation in there, did you, Tom?'

'Nay, sir.' Tom's flush deepened as his heart surged with pride.

Sir Francis chuckled. 'I didn't think so... Tell me, is Lord Monteagle often here at Essex House?'

'Aye, sir,' said Tom. 'Almost every day.'

'Really? And who else has the earl been playing host to recently?'

'Almost too many to keep count of, sir. Why these past few days alone, we have welcomed the Earls of Southampton, Rutland, Sussex and Bedford, and Lords Cromwell and Sandys.'

Sir Francis stopped in his tracks and stared at Tom. Then he raised his head and frowned, stroking his beard as if lost in thought. 'Very interesting,' he mused. 'You know, Tom, if I was to name the seven most impoverished nobles in all of England, it would have been those six you just mentioned, together with Lord Monteagle. All of them have spent their wealth recklessly, either in the pursuit of pleasure or in the hope of court favour, and they are now desperately short of money. They are men with nothing to lose, Tom, and men with nothing to lose can be very dangerous. I am surprised that your master would choose to keep such company.'

Tom did not know what to say to this. He felt honoured that Sir Francis would choose to share these thoughts with him, a lowly servant. It also scared him a little, if what Sir Francis said was true. Why indeed was the earl choosing such company? Could all this be part of his plan to take revenge on the Beagle?

They descended the main staircase in silence. Tom left Sir Francis in the lobby in order to fetch him his hat and cloak. When he returned, Sir Francis was nowhere to be seen.

Where has he got to? thought Tom. He searched the rooms adjoining the lobby, and eventually found him in the Picture Gallery, a long, oak-panelled room filled with the earl's most valuable paintings. Sir Francis was at the far end of the room with his back to Tom. He was studying one of the larger canvases, deep in thought. Tom was surprised to find Sir Francis here, looking so absorbed. A moment ago, he had seemed in such a hurry to leave.

The painting he was looking at was a portrait of two wealthy-looking young men. The men were leaning on a display cabinet, upon which had been placed an array of objects. It was a picture that had caught Tom's eye on previous visits to the room, mainly because of its rich detailing and the fascinating nature of the objects it depicted. There was also something very strange in the foreground of the painting – a grey, elongated shape rising up from the floor at an angle. Tom had always wondered what it was.

As he approached Sir Francis, the philosopher said, without turning around: 'You know, Tom, there are codes everywhere for those with eyes to see them – even in paintings.'

'Are there, sir?'

'Indeed! And if you can understand these codes, you can read a painting like a book. Take this one for example…' Sir Francis gestured towards the painting he'd been examining. 'Painted in 1533 by Hans Holbein, it's called *The Ambassadors*. What was going on in 1533, Tom? Do you know?'

'Er, that would have been during the reign of the queen's father, King Henry VIII, sir.'

'That's right. And King Henry broke with the Roman Church, didn't he, so that he could marry Anne Boleyn, the queen's mother.'

'Aye, sir. That was when England became a Protestant country.'

'Indeed, and not only England. In other parts of Europe, too, people were setting up Protestant Churches, free of the Pope's control. This painting is full of codes that speak of this time of division within the Church – the time we call the Reformation.'

Tom studied the painting with its two solemn men and the objects in the cabinet – the globes of the heavens and the Earth, the sundial, the musical instruments and the book. He searched for anything that might speak of the Reformation, but could find nothing.

Sir Francis pointed to the top left corner. 'See that crucifix half covered by a curtain,' he said. 'That represents the division of the Church.'

Tom hadn't even noticed the crucifix.

Sir Francis's pointing finger then moved to another part of the painting. 'And there, on the lower shelf of the cabinet, see the lute has a broken string, reflecting the disharmony that was felt by many at the time. Even the book of arithmetic is open on the page of division.'

Tom looked closer, and saw that he was right.

'There is more, much more, to be found here, if you look carefully. Keep your eyes open, my boy. You'll be surprised at what you see.'

Sir Francis stared closely at him, and his eyes seemed at once to twinkle like jewels and pierce like steel. Tom sensed that the philosopher was no longer talking about the painting. *Did he want him to be his spy?*

Suddenly, Tom didn't feel so comfortable. He tore free of Sir Francis's gaze. 'Tell me, sir,' he said distractedly, 'I have never understood what this is.' He pointed with a shaking finger at the strange, elongated shape sloping up from the floor in the foreground of the painting.

'That,' said Sir Francis, 'is the most interesting part of all. It puzzles everyone who looks at it. The mistake everyone makes, of course, is to view it in the same way as they view the rest of the painting – face on. What the artist is teaching us here is that some things can only be understood when looked at in a different way.'

'What way would that be, sir?'

Sir Francis went into a crouch close to the wall just below the painting. He peered up at it from a position low on its left-hand side. Then he beckoned to Tom. 'Come here. Take a look at it from this perspective.' Sir Francis moved out of the way, so Tom could take his place. Tom gazed up along the same slanted angle, and got a big surprise. From this foreshortened viewpoint it became obvious that the elongated shape was the distorted view of a familiar yet disturbing object.

'It's a skull,' he said.

'Indeed,' said Sir Francis. 'It reminds me of a line from the play *King Richard II* by William Shakespeare: 'Like perspectives, which rightly gazed upon / Show nothing but confusion, eyed awry / Distinguish form…'

'But why did the artist paint it in this way?'

'Why indeed? Perhaps because the skull is the symbol of death… something we do not care to think about too often in our daily lives – yet it's always there.'

As they made their way back to the lobby, Sir Francis said: 'Remember to keep your eyes open, Tom, and maybe... Well, let's just say that I hope I may have the pleasure of speaking with you again soon.'

'I hope so too, sir.'

Tom stood at the entrance of Essex House and watched as the little man, now wearing his cloak and tall black hat, made his way down to the riverbank where his personal barge was moored.

Chapter 4

Becoming Ophelia

Alice was covered in pig's blood. She was seated on a stool in the Props Room at the Globe scooping the thick, dark red liquid out of a bucket with a soup ladle and pouring it into a pig's bladder. It was hard to get the blood through the small hole in the bladder, so quite a lot of it had spilled onto her tunic. The blood, bladder and other animal parts had been delivered to the Globe that morning by a local butcher. This afternoon, the Chamberlain's Men were due to perform *The Tragedy of Hamlet* for the first time. There were to be four stabbings in the play, and the audience would expect to see plenty of blood flowing from each of them. The bladders would be secreted beneath the player's costumes, ready to be pierced by the points of swords during the stage fights.

Another reason for all the blood spillage on her clothes was that Alice was finding it hard to concentrate. Her mind was on her brother, who had been missing since Saturday afternoon. For much of yesterday she had searched for him in the taverns of the Paris Garden and Bankside. This morning she had questioned his friends here at the Globe. No one had seen or heard of him. Where had he gone? She wouldn't let herself imagine the worst – that he was lying dead somewhere. But what *was* she to imagine? Her stomach convulsed as more blood splashed onto her arm and trickled down to her wrist. It was cold and sticky.

Richard was due to play the role of Ophelia, and the play was starting in just three hours. It wasn't like him to run away from his responsibilities, no matter how nervous he was. If there was an explanation, she was sure it was to be found in the mysterious coded message that she'd discovered in the chest under his bed – a message she now carried with her everywhere, tucked inside her belt. Perhaps someone here could help her work out what it meant.

She was wondering who she might ask when the door suddenly opened and Augustine Phillips entered the room. He was a sharer – one of the eight men who shared the company's profits and debts. They formed the core of the Chamberlain's Men, and if there was a leading figure among them it was Augustine, known to his friends as Gus. He was a large man with a ruddy complexion and bushy beard. Being in his late forties, he tended to play the parts of older characters. Although he was not the most gifted player at the Globe, he was a brilliant organiser, and in charge of the company's money and props.

'Zounds!' he cried when he saw her. 'What a mess you are, boy! I trust at least some of the blood will end up in those bladders!'

'I'm doing my best, Mr Phillips.'

'Well, you can put that aside for now, as I have a new task for you – one that involves less blood and more tears.'

'What new task, sir?'

'I have met with the other sharers to discuss our present plight, and we have decided that we can wait no longer for your brother to appear. You, Adam, will play the role of Ophelia this afternoon!'

Alice was so shocked she dropped the ladle, which fell with a splosh into the bucket.

'Me, Mr Phillips?'

'Aye! You know the lines well enough. I saw you helping Richard with them on Saturday last. I think you'll make a very fine Ophelia.'

'But…'

'There's no time to lose, Adam. Come with me now to Wardrobe, and we can try you out in some dresses.'

'But, sir, I am no player. I'm a stagehand. I create the effects. I feed lines to players when they've forgotten them. I clean the playhouse after shows. My place is not on the stage.'

'In faith, you *have* been on stage!' Gus insisted. 'I've seen you there!'

'But only in very small parts, sir, and none that required a player's skill.'

Gus was fast losing patience. 'Your brother isn't here, and there's no one else I can turn to. You must step into the breach, Adam, and that is the end of it!'

Wardrobe was situated next door to the Props Room and above the Tiring-House. Alice normally loved her visits to Wardrobe. It was a musty-smelling jumble of racks and boxes containing robes, cloaks, doublets, hose, jerkins, togas, hats, dresses, wigs, jewellery, armour and fancy footwear. Some of the dresses were quite beautiful – studded with precious stones and trimmed with lace. There had been times when she found herself alone in the room and she would run her hands through the luscious velvet and silk fabric and imagine herself wearing such clothes.

Yet here she was today, actually being asked to try them on, and instead of joy, she felt terror – it was like a paralysing fear in the pit of her stomach.

Oh, Richard, Richard! Where are you?

Unlike her brother, she had never felt any desire to go on the stage. She was happy behind the scenes, rolling cannonballs around to make thunder, igniting firecrackers for lightning, and putting players in harnesses for special entrances from above the stage. She was prepared to play the odd minor role, if she was needed – but Gus had no right to make her play Ophelia. She was going to ruin the play!

Alice entered the room in time to witness Timothy, the wiry little props man, being barked at by a larger, stouter fellow wearing a fake gold crown. Alice recognised him as Henry Condell, one of the sharers.

'Call this a robe?' Condell shouted, eyeing the fur-lined garment dangling from his shoulders. 'It barely reaches my calves. I'm supposed to be Fortinbras, Prince of Norway, not some capering courtier. How am I supposed to look dignified in this?'

'Begging your pardon, Mr Condell, sir,' blushed Timothy, 'but it's the biggest one I have.'

'Fuss not, Harry,' said Gus, entering the room behind Alice. 'The grandeur of your performance will more than compensate for any shortness of robe.'

Henry left, still scowling and muttering, as Gus turned to the props man. 'Timothy. We need to turn this butcher's boy into Ophelia. Can you do that for me?'

'Aye, Mr Phillips, sir. Right away.'

'Good. I will be in rehearsals if you need me.'

As Alice washed herself in a bowl in the corner of the room, a new fear crept into her. In the few previous roles she had played on stage, she had always been a boy. If she was to dress up as a girl, wouldn't it become obvious to everyone that she was, in fact, *a girl?*

It would take just one loudmouth in an audience of

thousands to realise it – just one person to start up a chant (*She's a girl! She's a girl!*) – and her life would be over. She'd be thrown out of the Chamberlain's Men, and then what would become of her? She'd be back on the streets, and she'd miss Richard's return. She might never see her brother again!

Finding herself some privacy behind a tall clothes rack, Alice reluctantly slipped out of her blood-stained tunic and put on the first of the dresses that Timothy had laid out for her. Luckily, the props man was too busy with needle and thread, repairing another costume, to take much notice of her. She tried on three frocks in all, checking how she looked in each one in a tall looking-glass resting against the wall. Her favourite was a white linen dress with a simple, square neckline and loose sleeves. It seemed the right look, somehow, for the innocent young Ophelia. It also had the advantage of being long and loose-fitting, disguising her female shape.

'This one, I think, Timothy,' she said, stepping out shyly from behind the clothes rack.

Timothy looked her up and down and Alice tensed, fearing that he had spotted her femaleness. But all he said was: 'It's a little baggy, Adam. Would you like me to take it in at the waist? Or maybe give you a belt?'

'Oh no,' said Alice swiftly. 'I think it's fine like this.'

'Very well,' he said, still sounding uncertain. 'Shall we try on some wigs?'

Nervously, Alice seated herself on a stool before

another, smaller looking-glass, as Timothy rummaged in a box. 'We have the Anne Boleyn-style,' he said, holding up one with long, straight auburn tresses. 'You can have it plaited or in a bun.' He picked out another. 'Or this one's frizzy like Queen Bess.'

As he placed each wig over Alice's cropped, boyish hair, she trembled inside. When would he realise? She tried to make her face hard and masculine, pressing her lips together and sucking in her cheeks. So busy was she making faces in the looking-glass that she did not notice the arrival of another person in the room.

'Well met, Adam,' said a soft, low voice.

Alice turned. Will Shakespeare was standing over her.

Chapter 5

Mr Shakespeare

'Good day to you, sir,' said Alice. Her heart beat harder, as it always did in Will Shakespeare's presence. This had nothing to do with his appearance. He was a man of medium height with a high forehead and a neat beard. He might have been a clerk or a minor courtier. He certainly didn't have the forceful bearing of some of the other sharers, like Richard Burbage or Gus Phillips. Only the brightness of Shakespeare's gaze gave a clue to his genius. When he looked at her, Alice didn't feel he was merely *looking* – he was also thinking and reflecting on what he saw. It was as if his mind was constantly reimagining the world into words and scenes and plays. *We are all his material,* she sometimes thought.

Will plucked another wig from the box. 'Here, good Tim, try this one,' he said.

The hair on this wig was long and fair and fell in loose ringlets. Timothy placed it on her head, and the effect was dramatic. Alice's eyes widened. The face in the mirror was now unquestionably that of a girl, and a disturbingly pretty one. Her lips, her eyes, the way the ringlets fell around her face – they all betrayed her.

To her surprise, there were no gasps of shock from the other two. Either they did not see what she saw, or they were determined not to. Will only murmured: 'There she sits – a sad and fearful maid, pure of heart, torn between loyalty to her father and brother, and her love for Hamlet. Whatever is in your heart right now, Adam, remember it, for it makes the face of Ophelia.'

'I fear I will ruin your play, sir,' said Alice. 'I am not rehearsed.'

'Pray hold on to that fear then, if it begets such a face,' muttered Will, before adding with a rueful laugh: 'You will not ruin my play, Adam. Phillips, Condell and Heminges will do that well enough without any help from you. Do you recall Hamlet's advice to the players in Act Three?'

She began to quote it: '"Speak the speech, I pray you, as I pronounced it to you, trippingly on the tongue…"'

'Aye, well you can forget most of that,' chuckled Will. 'That was just my little dig at the vain, strutting, robustious fellows, of which there are more than several in our company. You are not of that ilk, Adam. If you should take anything from Hamlet's counsel, it would be this: "suit the action to the word, the word to the action". And remember that the whole purpose of playing is to hold "the mirror up to nature". In other words, be true to Ophelia.' He smiled. 'And, I beseech you, try not to trip over the scenery.'

After Will had departed, Alice pulled off the wig. She dearly wished she could take off the dress and get back into her boy-clothes.

'I hate this look,' she confided to Timothy.

'But it suits you, Adam,' he said, plucking the wig from her resisting hands and replacing it on her head. He adjusted it until he was satisfied. 'The butcher's boy has scrubbed up quite well!' he decided. 'Now, let's do something about those pink cheeks. If the audience are really to believe you a maiden, you must be pale.' Timothy found a jar of powdered hogs' bones mixed with poppy oil, which he proceeded to dab on her face, turning it almost white. He was putting the final touches to her make-up when she received the summons for rehearsals.

Alice braced herself as she walked down the steps and out onto the stage. This was the moment, surely, when the deception she had practised for the last two years would finally be exposed. But, as it turned out, the other players were too busy practising their moves or running through their lines to even notice her. Richard Burbage, who was to play Hamlet, was at the front of the stage, skull in hand, rehearsing a scene with a couple of the hired men. Alice was almost as starstruck by Burbage as she was by Shakespeare. He was for certain the most gifted player she had ever seen, able to memorise vast numbers of lines and deliver them with passion and sincerity as if they had just at that moment sprung from his heart. She had seen Burbage play the savage, fiery Tamburlaine, the noble Brutus, and the crook-backed schemer Richard III. But from what she had glimpsed during the rehearsals for Hamlet, this was to be his greatest performance yet.

Burbage spotted her watching him. He broke off in mid-speech and strolled over. 'How goes it, Adam? Very good of you to step in for your brother like this. Any word of him, by the way?'

'None, sir.'

'Ah, me!' he sighed. 'I fear the poor lad may have taken fright and gone into hiding somewhere. He won't be the first young player to suffer nerves before a performance, and he won't be the last. I dare say he'll reemerge sheep-faced tomorrow. Until then, you are free to steal his glory.' Burbage looked more closely at her. 'Tis no comfort to you, I'm sure, young Adam, but you do look the part – more than passingly so. In faith, if I didn't know better, I'd take you for a girl!'

Alice tried to laugh, but it came out more like a sob. 'Sh-Shall we rehearse, Mr Burbage?'

'Indeed! Let's do that.'

After an hour of intense rehearsing, Alice was permitted a short break while Burbage practised a sword fight with John Heminges, another player-sharer, who would be playing the part of Laertes. Their swords were wooden, but painted to look like metal. The fight was being directed by Robert Armin, another player-sharer, a former soldier. He was shouting instructions at them as they darted around the stage:

'Stramazone!' Armin roared, and Burbage swished his sword towards Heminges's head. Heminges managed to block. *'Punta riversa!'* cried Armin. Burbage took a step forwards, thrusting his sword, knuckles down, inside Heminges's guard. Heminges spun out of the way. Burbage was striking at his opponent with anger in his eyes, as if he meant to kill. *'Mandritta!'* bellowed Armin, and Burbage delivered a horizontal cut with palm upward, from right to left. This time, his sword struck Heminges on the side, making him cry out.

Alice spotted her friend Edmund Squires among a group of prentices watching the fight. Perhaps *he* would be able to help her decipher the mysterious note.

'Edmund!' she hissed, sneaking up beside him.

He turned. 'What ho, Adam.' He blinked in surprise when he saw her. But his attention was soon back on the clashing swords. 'By my troth, this is going to be some spectacle!' he exclaimed. She could see he was dazzled by the duel. It would be hard to drag him away.

'I need your help with something,' she said. 'Can you spare me a little time?'

'Is there news of your brother?' he asked, still distracted.

Alice shook her head sadly. 'Nay, but I have found something that may lead us to where he is.'

This caught his attention. 'Forsooth? Then come this way.' He led her into the Tiring-House.

Edmund was a few years older than Alice. An amiable, fair-haired youth, he had grown tall in recent months and his voice had deepened, making it harder for him to play female roles. He hoped soon to graduate from prentice to hired man, if the sharers agreed.

'My, you are a comely wench in that get-up, Adam,' smirked Edmund after shutting the door behind them. 'I could almost kiss you!'

'Away with you!' said Alice with a glare. 'I may look like a maid today, but these fists are still hard as cobble-stones, and I shall beat you with them if you don't be quiet.'

'I have great respect for your fists!' laughed Edmund. 'They have left a deep impression on me in the past! So what is it you have found that might lead you to Richard?'

Alice drew the note from her sleeve and handed it to him. 'This was among his possessions,' she said. 'Do you have any idea what it might mean?'

Edmund puzzled over the note. 'The horse and carriage could signify travel. Do you suppose Richard had to go somewhere?'

'He would have told me if so,' said Alice. 'If he went anywhere, it would have been against his will.'

'I dare say you are right,' frowned Edmund, and he studied the note some more. 'May I keep a hold of this?' he said at last. 'There could be some pattern buried within these nonsense letters. With further study, it's possible I might find it.'

'I cannot,' said Alice. 'Forgive me, Edmund. The note is all I have of Richard's, and I have vowed never to let it out of my hands.'

'I understand,' said Edmund, handing it back to her.

'Adam!' called Robert Armin from the doorway. 'We need you on the stage. Come quickly!'

Edmund smiled at her as she tucked the note hastily back inside her sleeve. 'I wish you luck for this afternoon, my friend,' he said. 'I will see you on stage!'

Chapter 6

Hamlet

Tom descended a set of narrow stone steps that led to the river's edge. He paid a few pennies to the waterman and stepped into his wherry-boat. The waterman cast off and began to row with steady strokes out into the river towards Southwark.

Tom sat in the stern and gripped the gunwhales, excitement bubbling up inside him. Sir Gelly had given him the afternoon off and he'd decided to go and see a play. Tom had never seen a play before, but some of the other servants had told him about them – about how sad, funny and sometimes violent stories were acted out by costumed players on a stage. It sounded wonderful!

The playhouses had a poor reputation among the officials who ran the City. They regarded them as rowdy, uproarious places – magnets for thieves, drunkards and other undesirables. So the playhouses had been forced to set up outside the City walls, in Southwark on the south bank of the Thames. This made the whole experience even more exhilarating for Tom. As he sat there in the boat, he pretended the Thames was an ocean, and he was an explorer, like Sir Walter Raleigh, setting out for a wild and lawless land on its distant shore.

The Thames could not easily be mistaken for an ocean today, for it was crowded with wherry-boats making the same journey from north to south across the choppy waters. It was slow-going, as they had to navigate around the much bigger coal barges, fishing vessels and cargo ships that glided up and down the middle of the river. To the east lay London Bridge, rising out of the grey river fog. The City's only bridge was crammed from one end to the other with houses and shops that seemed too heavy for its twenty pillars to bear.

At length, the waterman reached a jetty on the south bank. Tom thanked him and disembarked. He followed the stream of entertainment-seekers along a wide road that led them eastwards. Among the crowd, Tom spotted all types, from wealthy women with extravagant headdresses and hooped skirts to noisy groups of prentices enjoying their afternoon off. There were foreign tourists with long feathers in their felt hats, portly shopkeepers on a day out with their wives, and flamboyantly dressed young men in velvet doublets slashed to expose colourful silk linings. Beggar children ran around, barging into people and pleading for coins. A group of men were playing bowls on a dusty patch of ground next to a tavern. Nearby, some musicians were performing on the viol and the pipe, while another sang a ballad and held out his hat to the passersby.

As they drew nearer to the palaces of entertainment, the crowd – which by now was massive – split into separate streams. Those with a taste for a more violent kind of spectacle headed towards the bull-ring. Tom could hear the barking of the mastiffs, kept chained in kennels outside the amphitheatre. They used the dogs to bait the bulls, so he'd heard. He observed a beribboned horse with a monkey tied to its saddle being pulled through one of the entrances into the bull-ring – some sort of warm-up entertainment, he assumed.

Up ahead, he caught sight of his destination – the Globe. It had been built just two years ago, Sir Gelly had informed him, and in that time had acquired a reputation as the greatest playhouse of them all. From a distance, the building looked like a squat, circular tower with white, half-timbered walls and a thatched roof. As he came closer, he saw that it was not circular but made up of lots of flat sides. Tom took his place in the queue at the playhouse's entrance. Street vendors moved along the line with their baskets of goods.

'Ripe pippins, ripe, to win your true-love's heart!'

'Nuts. Fine nuts. Hazelnuts. Tuppeny a pound.'

His excitement mounted as he finally reached the head of the queue and pushed his way through the narrow entrance into the dim lobby. A pair of wealthy ladies ahead of him paid several pennies and mounted some steps that led to the expensive seats in the upper gallery. Tom, on a servant's wage, couldn't afford such luxuries. He took a penny from the leather purse attached to his belt and handed it to the gatherer. Then he began to shuffle forwards, his progress slowed by the dense throng of people ahead of him.

Eventually, he emerged into the Globe's central yard. It was open to the sky and surrounded on all sides by galleries of seating now filling up with the richer members of the audience. A raised stage projected out into the yard, covered by a roof supported by two colourful pillars. The ceiling above the stage was decorated with depictions of the sun and signs of the zodiac painted on a deep blue background, reminding Tom of the celestial globe in *The Ambassadors* painting back at Essex House. At the rear of the stage were several doorways that, he guessed, led to rooms where the players waited to come on. Above this were balconies where finely dressed lords and ladies sat like beautiful birds on display. *Those must be the best seats in the house,* thought Tom.

He felt hemmed in on all sides by the smelly, noisy crowd. There were more vendors inside the yard loudly hawking their fruit and leather bottles of ale. Tom kept his eyes fixed on the doors at the back of the stage, waiting for them to open. Things would quieten, he hoped, when the play began.

And then, above the shouts, the laughter and the crackle of hundreds of nutshells, he heard the high-pitched blare of a trumpet. The crowd barely quietened as the stage door swung open and a man stepped out. He was dressed like a guard in a leather jerkin and helmet, a sword hanging from his belt. After the guard had taken up a position near the front of the stage, another one emerged, dressed identically. He called out to the first: 'Who's there?'

The first guard turned in alarm, drawing his sword and shouting: 'Nay, answer me: stand, and unfold yourself.'

'Long live the king!'

'Bernado?'

'He.'

The men were speaking these words at the tops of their voices, yet Tom struggled to hear their conversation above the hubbub in the yard. Nevertheless, he could see from their movements and expressions that both men were jumpy and afraid. He found out why a short while later, after two more players entered, and one of them asked: 'What, has this thing appear'd again to-night?' Tom quickly worked out that they were speaking of a ghost that had been visiting the guards on their watch.

A hush finally stole over the crowd as another door opened and a man in armour advanced slowly onto the stage. His face and beard were perfectly white

– he had to be the ghost! The other men on the stage cringed in fear when they saw the apparition: '… look, where it comes again!' said one.

'In the same figure, like the king that's dead,' said another.

By now, Tom had forgotten that he was watching a play. He had forgotten everything and was completely caught up in the action on the stage. That was a ghost up there, without question, and those guards were real people suffering real terror.

The play progressed, and the story gradually became clearer to Tom. The king of Denmark had died, and his son, Prince Hamlet, had returned home from abroad to attend his father's funeral. Hamlet was shocked to learn that his mother was now married to his father's brother, Claudius, who had crowned himself king. The ghost of the dead king, Hamlet's father – the one from the opening scene – now reappeared and told Hamlet that Claudius had killed him, and Hamlet must avenge his death, or else he would be forced to walk the earth alone for eternity.

Tom waited excitedly for Hamlet to kill his uncle, and was surprised when, instead, Hamlet hesitated. The prince started to question whether the ghost really was his father – might it not, in fact, be an agent of the devil? Then Hamlet started to question himself, wondering if his hesitation was a mark of cowardice. He behaved strangely: he pretended to be mad so that he could observe Claudius without attracting suspicion. He commissioned a troupe of players to perform a play in which a king is killed so that he could observe its effect on his uncle. Hamlet, Tom soon realised, was a man of words, rather than deeds. Tom felt frustrated by him, but also intrigued. On several occasions, Hamlet spoke his thoughts aloud to the audience. It was fascinating to be able to listen in to the thoughts of another human being.

But it wasn't only the character of Hamlet that had snared Tom's attention. He also found himself captivated by Ophelia, the young woman who Hamlet was in love with. Tom had been warned by the other servants that women were forbidden from performing on the stage and that all the female parts were played by boys or young men. He could certainly believe this in the case of the queen, Gertrude, a tall and quite muscular lady whose chin was showing signs of stubble, despite her heavy make-up. Ophelia, however, looked every inch a maid, and an extremely pretty one too. She spoke her lines quietly, and seemed more nervous than her fellow players. Yet she had a special quality – both mysterious and sad – and when she was on the stage, he could scarcely take his eyes off her.

Engrossed as he was in the drama on the stage, Tom didn't notice at first when someone in the crowd suddenly jostled him. It hadn't been the first time he'd been pushed around while standing there in the yard. Every few minutes, he was caught in a ripple of movement passing through the close-packed crowd. But this time it felt different – less random. He sensed a disturbing lightness around his belt, and glanced down. A frayed leather string hung there.

His purse was gone!

Chapter 7

Stage Fright

In a panic, Tom looked around and spotted someone in a felt copotain – a conical hat – moving swiftly away from him towards the playhouse exit. He charged after him.

'Out of my way!' he shouted as he tried to shoulder his way through the press.

That purse contained his week's wages – and the coins he needed to pay the waterman to take him back across the river!

By the time he made it to the exit and pushed through the doors to the street, the cutpurse was nowhere to be seen. 'Gog's Blood!' yelled Tom, kicking angrily at the wall of the playhouse. *What was he to do?*

All the excitement he'd felt just moments ago had

drained away. He no longer had any appetite to watch the play and find out the fate of Hamlet, Ophelia, Claudius and the rest – now he only wanted to go home, and that meant a long and dreary walk via London Bridge. He was starting to make his way in that direction when he was arrested by a shout.

'Young sir!'

Tom turned to see a middle-aged woman – one of the fruit vendors – looking his way. She grinned at him, displaying a mouth with just three or four teeth. 'You lost your purse, methinks.'

Tom nodded.

'I seen a man wearin' one of them copotain hats with a purse in his hand. He went that way.' She pointed along the wall of the playhouse.

'Thank you, mistress!' Tom shouted to her, as he sped off in that direction.

Towards the rear of the building, he came upon the thief, crouching down, his back against the wall, pouring the coins out of the leather purse into his palm.

'Rogue!' cried Tom, running at him.

The thief leapt up in alarm, and took off at a sprint. But Tom was faster, and closing in on him with every second. Aware of Tom breathing down his neck, the cutpurse pulled open a door set into the wall of the playhouse and ducked inside. Tom followed after him, and found himself in a cramped, gloomy space full of strange objects.

'You can't hide from me you scoundrel,' he growled

as he peered behind a wooden rainbow and lifted up a bearskin. He pushed aside several shields and kicked over a cauldron, but there was no sign of his quarry.

Where had the man gone?

The sound of a creaking hinge made him look up. Tom dashed through the closing door into another room. He nearly tripped over some clothing draped on the floor. The thief was nowhere to be seen. There was only one other door he could have escaped through and that lay straight ahead. Tom barged through it and ran forward a few paces. Then he stopped, and blinked. He was in sunlight. A sea of faces gazed up at him from the yard – and down upon him from the galleries. He was on the stage!

Hamlet and Gertrude were there, too, both startled by this unexpected arrival. Gertrude, staring at him, cried out: 'What wilt thou do? Thou wilt not murder me? Help, ho!'

What was the woman thinking?

'By all the gods, of course I will not!' Tom assured her, and he was surprised that this provoked laughter from the audience. He began backing towards the door he had just come through. 'Forgive me,' he mouthed to the players.

Then a voice called out behind him: 'What, ho! Help!'

Tom spun around to see an older man crouching behind a curtained screen placed near the door. He recognized him as Polonius, the father of Ophelia. Polonius was also staring at Tom.

'Fear not, I mean you no harm!' Tom assured him.

Then Hamlet drew his sword, crying 'How now! a rat? Dead, for a ducat, dead!'

At first, Tom thought that Hamlet was about to attack him. But instead, he went for Polonius. To Tom's horror, Hamlet thrust his sword through the curtain and right into the old man's heart. Blood spurted from Polonius's chest as he came staggering onto the stage, groaning 'O, I am slain!' before collapsing in a heap.

'O me, what hast thou done?' wailed Gertrude.

'Murder!' bawled Tom. 'That's what he's done! Foul murder!'

He couldn't understand why Gertrude was frantically gesturing at him – nor why the audience was now howling with laughter. Did no one realise that a man had just been killed?

Hamlet was glaring furiously at Tom, and Tom began to fear that he might be his next victim. Then he felt someone tugging at his boot. He looked down. It was Polonius, still clinging to life. The old man was mouthing words at him. Was he asking for a physician? No, he was saying: 'Get off the stage!'

And then Tom felt a prickle of dawning awareness. This was all an act! The blood was fake! Polonius was fine! He looked out across the cackling hordes of spectators and wanted only to disappear. Mortified, he dashed through the nearest door and off the stage.

But the door he fled through was different from the one he'd come in by. It took him into a very small room

– not much more than a landing – with a set of spiral stairs heading to places above and below.

'Remove that intruder!' thundered a voice from above, quickly followed by a clatter of heavy boots descending.

Tom's only option was to flee downwards. The journey ended after just five or six steps. He found himself in a low-ceilinged basement area supported by wooden posts. All was dark, save for the weak flame of a single rushlight perched in an iron stand on the floor. Something was illuminated by its glow. Tom shook with fright when he saw that it was the white face of the ghost.

Chapter 8

A Visit to Hell

The ghost wasn't looking at Tom. It was standing in a crouched posture on a set of steps, struggling with something on the ceiling. And there was someone else with the ghost – Ophelia! Tom's heart nearly stopped beating when he saw her there. Her face was tilted upwards, attention focused on whatever it was the ghost was battling with.

Tom edged closer to them – somehow, for he could no longer feel his legs.

'The bolt is stuck fast,' the ghost was saying.

'Let *me* try, Mr Shakespeare,' said Ophelia.

The ghost shifted to one side. Ophelia mounted the first of the steps and reached up to the same place in the low ceiling.

'A fine spirit am I who cannot even pass through a flimsy trapdoor,' moaned the ghost, as Ophelia fought to open the bolt.

From above, Tom could hear the squeak of boots on the stage and the muffled voices of Hamlet and Gertrude.

So, they were now directly beneath the stage. Was the ghost planning to rise up out of that trapdoor? He wished he could be back in the audience, just to see such a thing!

'It is nearly your cue to enter, Mr Shakespeare,' panted Ophelia. She was having no more luck with the bolt than the ghost had. As she struggled, something fell from her sleeve and fluttered to the ground near to where Tom was standing. He stooped and picked it up. It was a small scroll, partly opened. In the dim light he saw, in the corner, the figure of a leopard's head upon a fleur de lys. He'd recognise that symbol anywhere: it was Lord Monteagle's family crest. So was this girl – he still couldn't bring himself to think of her as a boy in disguise – related to Monteagle? Might she, too, be a Catholic?

He stepped out of the shadows. 'My lady,' he said, handing it to her. 'You dropped this.'

Ophelia stopped what she was doing and stared at him. So did the ghost.

'Who are you?' asked the girl, snatching the scroll from him and stuffing it back into her sleeve.

'I am…' He was so nervous, he momentarily forgot his name. 'I am Tom, my lady.'

'And what is your purpose here, Tom?' asked the ghost.

Tom tried to control his breathing.

'I am…' *What could he say*? And then he brightened as an idea came to him. 'I am here, sir, to free that bolt.'

The ghost nodded. 'Then pray do so, that I may free this spirit. For I am right now in *hell*.'

Tom thought this was overstating things slightly.

Ophelia, catching his frown, explained: 'We call this place beneath the stage "Hell". Mr Shakespeare was making a play on words – as is his habit.'

'Nay, Adam. I do not jest. I *am* in hell. Did you not hear the laughter from the groundlings just now? A bigger laugh I never heard for any comedy I wrote – and this is *not* a comedy.' He shoved Tom towards the steps. 'Get to it, boy, for if that bolt does not *open*, my Hamlet will *close* this very afternoon.'

'You wrote this play, sir?' asked Tom, reaching up and trying to yank open the bolt. 'Why, it is the best I have ever seen!'

'And how many have you seen?'

Tom was grateful for the shadows that cloaked his blushes. 'It is my first, I admit, sir. Yet even so, I doubt I will see a better one if I live to fifty.'

'If you live to fifty, Tom, you'll outlive this play and any other I care to write. They were *laughing*, I tell you, laughing at the death of Polonius!'

Again Tom blushed. 'That was *my* fault, sir. Just now, I strayed on to the stage by accident, and mistook the old man's play-acting for the truth. I feared Hamlet had really killed him.'

'You…' Mr Shakespeare spluttered. Then he began to chuckle. To Tom's discomfort, even Ophelia could not resist smiling. 'You really thought him killed, Tom?' laughed Shakespeare, wiping his teary eyes and smudging his white make-up. 'I confess I am much surprised. I did not think that Gus, who played Polonius, had such acting in him.'

Tom covered his embarrassment by putting renewed energy into opening the bolt – but it was harder to shift than he had anticipated.

'Hark!' cried Ophelia. 'It is your cue, Mr Shakespeare.'

Above them, Hamlet was saying: 'A cutpurse of the empire and the rule, That from a shelf the precious diadem stole, And put it in his pocket!'

'No more!' wept Gertrude.

'A king of shreds and patches—' said Hamlet.

There was an uncomfortable silence, as the players stood about, waiting for the ghost to appear.

'Hurry!' urged Ophelia from below. She touched the rushlight to a bowl of powder at the foot of the steps, and thick yellow smoke began to swirl around the basement.

Coughing, Tom pulled on the bolt until his fingers screamed. Finally, with a groan, it slid back.

Mr Shakespeare, still trying to suppress his giggles, nodded his thanks to Tom, pushed open the trapdoor and emerged onto the stage, surrounded by billowing clouds of the yellow smoke. Tom heard the gasps and screams of the audience.

'Come,' said Ophelia, leading him away from the smoky area around the trapdoor steps. When they were a safe distance away, she thanked him: 'Gramercy, Tom. You've saved the play!'

'It was the least I could do after nearly ruining it.' He wiped the sweat from his forehead.

'Now I must go,' she said, making for the stairs that led back to the ground floor. 'I must get cleaned up before my mad scene.'

'Mad scene?'

'I'm afraid so. Ophelia goes mad with grief over her father's death and Hamlet's mistreatment of her. I shall put flowers in my hair and sing sad love songs as I drown myself.'

'I'm sorry for you,' said Tom, awkwardly. 'I–I mean *her*.'

'Hey-ho,' she said. 'It's not a cheerful play – despite your efforts.' She smiled, but Tom saw little joy in it. The girl really did seem sad – like her character. He wished he could cheer her up.

'I thought you were… the best of all the players,' he said timidly.

'Go to!' she snorted. 'I was terrible. I only learned I was to play the role this morning.'

'How so?'

'My brother was to be Ophelia. But he vanished two days ago. So I was obliged to take his place.'

'I hope you find your brother.'

'Aye.' She looked at her feet. 'Well, I really should be going…'

'Wait!' cried Tom, not wanting their conversation to end.

She turned back from the stairs and waited for him to speak.

'How did they let you perform?' he asked.

'Why should they not?'

'You're a girl… aren't you?'

She looked up sharply, a deep frown denting her forehead. 'Are you so fooled by appearances, Tom? No, I am not a girl.' Her expression became mocking. 'I suppose if you could believe that Polonius was really murdered, then I should not be too surprised. This is your first play, after all.'

With that, she twisted away from him and hastened up the steps. Tom ran to the foot of the stairway and called up to her: 'Do you know Lord Monteagle?'

She peered down. 'Nay. Why do you ask?'

'That scroll you keep in your sleeve. It bears his crest.'

She stared at him, open-mouthed. It was not the reaction he had expected.

Slowly, she returned down the steps. With trembling fingers, she dug the scroll out of her sleeve, opened it and showed him the insignia. 'You mean this, with the leopard's head? How do you know?'

'He is a friend of my master's. I see him almost

every day, and he always wears that crest.'

Heavy footsteps sounded above and a player loomed into view. He leaned down into the basement, red-faced and panting. 'You!' he shouted at Tom. 'You shouldn't be here. This place is for players and stagehands only. Get out!'

Tom shrugged at Ophelia and began making his way back up the stairs.

'Stop!' she gasped. 'What is the name of your master?'

'The Earl of Essex,' he called back to her.

'Where does he live?'

'At Essex House, on the Strand.'

'Come on!' scowled the player, yanking Tom by the collar. He pushed him through a door and out onto the street. Tom turned to see the door slamming shut behind him. His mind was bursting with questions.

Why had she reacted that way when he'd explained the crest in her note, and why was she so interested in who his master was?

As he embarked on his long walk home, he had the feeling this wasn't the last he would be seeing of Ophelia.

Act Two

3rd February 1601

Chapter 9

Expedition

A thin drizzle fell on the yard of the Globe playhouse. It fell on the mounds of hazelnut shells and on the apple cores and the discarded bottles. It turned the ashen floor into a sticky mush that gummed up the boots of the prentices, who were hard at work cleaning up after yesterday's show. They had to drag the debris from the middle of the yard into piles at its edges. The piles would then be loaded onto wheelbarrows and taken away to be dumped in the river.

Alice, back in her boy-clothes and feeling rather cold and wet, tugged her broom through the mess. This was a far cry from yesterday, when she was up there on the stage in front of thousands, singing songs and going sweetly mad with flowers in her hair.

What a strange life she led!

'Good morrow, Adam!'

She looked up to see Gus Phillips smiling at her from the stage. 'You were uncommonly convincing as a maid, yesterday!' He said this with a smirk that did not leave her feeling entirely comfortable. Had he guessed the truth? If so, why did he not just come out and say it?

'Thank you, Mr Phillips,' she said, keeping her expression neutral.

'We're putting on Ben Jonson's play, *Every Man In His Humour*, tomorrow,' said Gus. 'It was a big success for us a few years ago, so we're reviving it. I've put you down to play Mistress Bridget. Once you've finished up here, you can have the rest of the day to yourself to study your lines.'

'Th-Thank you, sir,' replied Alice, flushing.

'Be back here tomorrow morning at nine for rehearsals.'

She watched Gus retreat into the Tiring-House, painfully aware of the jealous glares she was receiving from the other prentices. Most of them were older than her, and had served longer with the Chamberlain's Men – yet Alice was suddenly being offered the prize roles. She felt embarrassed, and sorry for the others. The only reason why she was being preferred was because her brother – the most talented of all the prentice-players – was missing, and she looked vaguely like him. Also, she hadn't completely disgraced herself as Ophelia yesterday. She wanted to tell the other prentices that none of this was her doing – she didn't even want to play these parts – but she suspected they wouldn't believe her, or if they did it would only increase their resentment. So, instead, she put her head down and continued sweeping.

If there was anything to please her about Gus's announcement, it was that she would get some time off. A prentice-player's day was normally spent performing menial tasks like cleaning the playhouse, hauling scenery, writing out roles for the players and maintaining and repairing props. When they weren't doing any of that, they were receiving lessons in stagecraft, fencing or how to apply make-up. The chance to avoid all of that, even for a single afternoon, was extremely welcome – especially as it gave Alice the chance to continue her search for Richard. She had a clue now, thanks to the boy, Tom, who had accidentally wandered backstage yesterday. Perhaps Richard had been kidnapped by this Lord Monteagle and was being held at Essex House. Perhaps she could go there this afternoon. If she loitered around the servants' entrance she might just learn something.

Then she remembered that she'd been given the afternoon off to learn her lines. But she could do that this evening, couldn't she? After all, hadn't she memorised the part of Ophelia accidentally while helping Richard? She obviously had a knack for that kind of thing. She would learn the part of Mistress Bridget tonight in her bedroom. Mrs Fairfax was a sound sleeper and hopefully wouldn't notice the candlelight, nor overhear Alice's mumbled efforts to fix the lines in her memory.

After the yard had been cleared and the brooms put away, the prentices gathered in one of the back rooms behind the Tiring-House for their luncheon of cold meat, carrots and clap bread. Edmund Squires found a place on the bench next to Alice. His habitual grin seemed even broader than usual.

'What ho, Adam. How goes it?'

'Well, Edmund.'

'My compliments to you for landing the part of Mistress Bridget! You are fast becoming a leading light among us prentice-players.'

'I am fast becoming a figure of hate,' answered Alice with a glance around the table at the others. No one but Edmund had spoken a word to her since Gus's announcement.

'Nonsense my good fellow,' said Edmund. 'No one who witnessed your Ophelia yesterday could deny that you deserve this. Watching you from the wings, I almost forgot you were a boy!'

Alice took a deep gulp of her ale to cover her embarrassment.

'And how do *you* fare, Edmund?' she hiccupped, eager to change the subject.

'Extremely well!' he beamed. 'I spoke this morning with Mr Phillips, and he assured me there is every chance that I will soon be appointed a hired man.'

'Truly? Edmund that is marvellous!'

She tried to sound enthusiastic, but it was hard, for there was so much else on her mind. Perhaps this was obvious from her expression, because Edmund's smile quickly disappeared. 'Still no word of your brother I take it?' he enquired.

'Nothing,' she said. 'Edmund, I am starting to fear that –'

'Nay!' he cried. 'You must not give way to such thoughts. We have to believe that he is alive, and go on believing that until we have proof to the contrary.'

Alice nodded. Edmund was right. They had to remain hopeful. Lowering her voice, she said: 'I have discovered something relating to that note I showed you.'

He glanced at her, eyebrows raised, and Alice told him what she had learned the day before from Tom. 'I will go to Essex House this afternoon and see what I can find out,' she concluded.

Edmund looked surprised. 'But do you not need to learn your lines for *Every Man In His Humour*?'

'I can do that this evening,' she said.

Still he looked pensive. 'I don't know, Adam. It sounds to me a perilous venture. You may be caught prowling and be clapped in irons...'

'I will take care not to be caught.'

'It does seem a very small clue on which to base so dangerous an expedition.'

'It's the only clue I have,' she said, a little disappointed by his reaction. 'Edmund, do you not see? I must follow every lead, no matter how small. Richard would do as much for me.'

Edmund pondered this a while, then his face broke into a smile. 'Marry, you speak the truth! And I was a fool to suggest otherwise. Of course you must go to Essex House. And I will accompany you there. It will be safer if we do this together.'

'Oh no, Edmund, I couldn't ask this of you!' she protested – though secretly she was delighted. It would be so much better to have a friend along.

'It would be a pleasure,' he said. 'I, too, have a free afternoon. For I am to play Roger Formal in *Every Man* – a part I know every line of, having understudied it the last time we performed the play.'

They set off soon after lunch. By now the rain had stopped and a weak sun was lancing through the clouds above the trees and meadows to the south. It shone on the cobbles and on the damp red-tiled roofs, and twinkled on the green surface of the Thames. They walked west along the river through Bankside and the Paris Garden until they reached a set of stone steps that led down to a jetty where the watermen waited with their wherry-boats. The river was at low tide and a grey beach extended from the bottom of the wooden pilings that formed the bank.

'What is that down there?' asked Edmund.

Alice had been distracted by the sight of a gilded barge carrying some important dignitary along the river. 'What is what?' she asked.

Edmund pointed to the beach below them. 'Someone has dropped something. It looks valuable.'

Now she saw it, lying on the sand, close to the steps: a silver object glinting in the shadows.

They continued down the steps to the beach. As she knelt to pick it up, a terrible chill entered her bones and her breath stopped in her throat. It was as if someone had plunged her into the cold river and held her down beneath the dark waters.

With desperate motions, she wiped the grains of sand off the surface of the locket. There was no mistaking the design of the engraving. Her fingers were trembling so much she could barely prise open the little case. Finally it opened, and the face of her mother looked back at her.

'I say, the lady in there looks like you,' remarked Edmund.

Alice dropped the locket and collapsed onto the beach. 'No, no, no!' she sobbed. 'It can't be!'

'Adam, what is it?' she heard Edmund gasp.

She couldn't answer – couldn't tell him that this was the proof she had been dreading. Richard was gone, drowned in the river, and his locket had washed up on the beach. All she could do now was cry – cry for her lost brother – and her tears seeped into the cold sand.

Chapter 10

The Beagle

Tom was coming down the main staircase when the doors of Essex House swung open and the yeomen of the guard came marching in. Tom stared in awe at the endless stream of plumed black hats and gold-embroidered scarlet tunics pouring into the lobby. The soldiers carried swords in their belts and long, gleaming, spear-like halberds across their shoulders. Trooping in two abreast, the column seemed endless. When the last ones had finally entered, the yeomen formed an open square around the edges of the lobby, facing the entrance. A moment later, three figures, all dressed in black with large silk ruffs, strode in. The middle figure was a very short man with a very long face, made even longer by his pointed beard and swept-back hair. He had thin unsmiling lips and dark raptor's eyes that roved restlessly about the room.

Tom was in little doubt as to the identity of this tiny, strange-looking man: it was, he was sure, Robert Cecil, chief minister and the most powerful person in England after the queen – the man they called the Beagle.

One of the black-robed attendants announced Lord Cecil's arrival to the porter, who scurried away with the news. Moments later, Sir Gelly Meyrick, the steward, appeared in the lobby, looking nervous and flustered.

'Good morrow, your grace,' he said with an awkward bow. 'The earl is most honoured to receive you. May I enquire as to the, uh…'

The chief minister's nostrils flared impatiently. 'Lord Monteagle is here, is he not?' He swivelled slowly, peering into every corner of the room as if hoping to discover Monteagle cowering beneath a chair or behind a suit of armour. 'I smell a plot,' said the Beagle, 'and whenever there is a plot, Monteagle is involved, one way or another. I want to question him. Bring him to me.'

Monteagle? Tom seemed to hear about him everywhere these days. Two days ago, Sir Francis had confided to Tom that Monteagle was a desperate man – one of the seven most impoverished nobles in England. Yesterday, Monteagle's crest had shown up on that note belonging to Ophelia. And now the Beagle was after him.

'Lord Monteagle isn't here, your grace,' said Sir Gelly, staring straight ahead.

'Then where is he?' snapped Cecil. 'He isn't at his house, nor at his favourite tavern, and when he isn't at either of those places, he is almost always here.'

'Forgive me, I am not privy to his movements,' said Sir Gelly.

At this point, the Earl of Essex entered from the Great Hall at the far end of the lobby. 'Cecil!' he cried. 'What a pleasure! Is this a social call? Have you been offered wine?'

The chief minister frowned. 'I have no desire to drink wine with you, Devereux!'

Essex nodded slowly, still smiling. Most people did not dare call him by his surname – but the Beagle was not 'most people'. The earl came closer, forcing the much shorter Cecil to raise his head to keep eye contact with him. 'How fares the queen?' Essex asked him. 'Does she ever speak of me?'

'Only with anger and bitterness,' spat Cecil. 'You have vexed her greatly, Devereux. But I'm not here about that. I want Monteagle. Where are you hiding him?'

'What makes you think he is here?' asked Essex coolly.

'My spies keep me informed of his movements. I know he has spent much time here of late.'

Essex gave a nonchalant shrug. 'I know nothing of his whereabouts.'

'In that case, you will not object if I conduct a search of your house.'

Tom now saw a flicker of unease in the earl's eyes. He was certain that the Beagle had seen it, too. Yet Essex maintained his cheerful demeanour. 'Of course. I have nothing to hide. Just tell your men to take care. I own some valuable Venetian glassware and Flemish tapestries, not to mention a collection of priceless paintings…'

Cecil ignored this. He was already instructing his attendants to organise the search.

Meanwhile, Essex, with Sir Gelly in his wake, headed for the great hall. Before departing the lobby, Sir Gelly noticed Tom on the staircase and beckoned him to follow. Tom dashed down the steps, squeezing past several red-coated yeomen, and hurried to catch up with the earl and his steward. The three of them exited the hall and entered the kitchens. In the pantry, amid the baskets of fruit, cheeses and plucked poultry, they found Lord Monteagle, sitting disconsolately on an upturned milk pail.

He jumped as they came in, then breathed a sigh of relief. 'It's the Beagle, isn't it?' he said.

'Aye,' said Essex. 'And he wants you.'

Monteagle looked forlorn. With his noble air and silken beard, he seemed out of place in this humble setting. 'I have been so careful over the years to cover my tracks,' he said. 'Though the Beagle always suspects me of treason, he can never find proof. Now, I wonder… Perhaps he has found something this time.'

'I doubt it,' said Essex. 'I believe his plan is merely to scare us. Even so, it would be better if you left. I have just told him that you aren't here. If he finds you, I could lose face…'

'And I could lose my *head*!' said Monteagle grimly.

'The door at the back of the pantry leads to the kitchen yard,' said Essex. 'From there it's a short walk to the river. I'll have a boat waiting for you.'

'They'll catch me for sure,' sighed Monteagle. 'I may have a quick mind, Robert, but I have slow feet. Is there not somewhere in this house where I can hide until they leave?'

Essex stroked his beard for a moment, then looked up. 'Maybe there is… As you know, this house once belonged to a prominent Catholic family. In the 1580s, they built a priest hole in the Picture Gallery. The family priest would hide there when the pursuivants came calling. The hideout is still there. The problem is, I'm not sure where. It's very well-hidden…'

'I believe I know where it is, my lord,' broke in Sir Gelly. 'The old steward told me on the day we moved in. He said the clue is in that painting, which you bought from the previous owner – *The Ambassadors*…'

Tom's ears pricked up when he heard this. Sir Francis had said there were secrets in that painting that even he hadn't discovered yet. Maybe he was right.

'There's a number hidden in that painting somewhere,' frowned Sir Gelly. 'It's a number between one and thirty. I know that because there are thirty paintings in the room, and the number refers to one of them. Whichever painting it is, the priest hole is beneath it. We just need to find the number.'

'Can't we just look behind each of the paintings?' asked Lord Monteagle anxiously. 'This is hardly the time to go hunting for hidden numbers.'

Sir Gelly shook his head. 'The priest hole is very well disguised within the wall panelling, my lord. It is the work of the master priest hole designer, Nicholas Owen. You would have to give the wall beneath each of the thirty paintings a thorough examination. It would take too long and is bound to attract the suspicions of the yeomen. Trust me, my lord, I am certain that when I look at *The Ambassadors*, I will find the number we seek.'

The stomp of approaching bootsteps made Monteagle leap up in fright.

'Take him there now, Sir Gelly,' instructed Essex.

'Aye, my lord,' said the steward and he quickly led the terrified Monteagle through the door at the rear of the pantry. As it was swinging shut, the door from the kitchen opened. In marched half a dozen yeomen, followed by the small, spider-like figure of Robert Cecil.

Tom hastily backed out of the way of the yeomen, but Essex stood his ground.

'How goes the search, Cecil?' he enquired calmly.

'Why are you hiding in here?' demanded the Beagle.

'I am not *hiding*!' said Essex, now indignant. 'Just keeping out of your way. The noise of your men is giving me a headache.'

Cecil ignored him. He was busy scouring the room with his hawk-eyes. They lit upon Tom, who had taken up a defensive position behind a large ham.

'You, boy,' he said, pointing at Tom with a long, crooked finger. 'Step closer so I can see you.'

His skin tingling, Tom edged into the middle of the room.

'What's a liveried boy like you doing in the pantry? Your domain is in the house, serving your master and his guests.'

'I – I was sent here,' said Tom.

'For what purpose?'

'I can answer that,' interjected Essex.

Cecil narrowed his eyes at the earl. 'If it pleases your lordship,' he said with exaggerated politeness, 'I would rather hear the boy speak.'

Tom was painfully aware that every eye in the room was upon him. It reminded him, in some ways, of his experience on the stage of the Globe yesterday, only that had merely been embarrassing – this was a matter of life and death. His next words were crucial.

'M-My master wished me to convey a, uh… message to the cook that there would be – that there would be some… extra guests for the banquet this evening. And now my master has come here because… because he wished to make a personal inspection of the pantry to ensure that the food to be served was of a decent standard… your grace.'

Essex was beaming at Tom as he said this, and he felt the beginnings of a warm glow inside. *He had done well!*

'I assumed you would be staying to dine with us later, Cecil,' put in Essex. 'I only wanted the best for you.'

The Beagle glared at him furiously. 'I am not a fool, Devereux,' he hissed, 'so don't play me for one. I know that Catholic renegade Monteagle is here somewhere in this house. It's only a matter of time before I find him.'

With that, he turned on his heel and marched out, trailed by his yeomen companions.

As soon as the door closed, Essex strode over to Tom and gave him a congratulatory slap on the back. 'That was quick thinking, young Tom,' he twinkled. 'You dug us out of a tight hole. When all this is over and I am back at court, I will see to it that you are amply rewarded.'

'Thank you my lord,' gulped Tom.

Robert Cecil and his men remained at Essex House for the whole morning and early afternoon, but they were unable to locate Lord Monteagle. At last, the chief minister called a halt to the search and his attendants assembled the yeomen in the courtyard.

They were watched by Essex's own 'rag-tag army' of soldiers, mercenaries and veterans of Ireland mostly, gathered in groups around the courtyard. The men had matted beards and shabby oxhide jerkins and rust-spotted swords.

'You haven't heard the last of this,' the Beagle warned Essex as he watched his beautifully dressed yeomen march in neat ranks through the main gate. Mounted on his mighty black steed, the little man was able, for once, to look down on the earl, and he seemed to relish it. 'I have left eight yeomen here in your household, and they will inform me immediately if Monteagle should show up, or miraculously appear from within the woodwork.'

'Of course,' said Essex drily. 'And of course I shall provide them with hospitality, free of charge, from my pantry, even though you have seen fit to impoverish me by withdrawing my licence for sweet wines.'

'That was the queen's decision.'

'And who has the queen's ear these days, Cecil?'

The Beagle curled his lip contemptuously. 'You're not doing too badly, Devereux, with your Venetian glassware and your Flemish tapestries, not to mention your priceless paintings.'

'So now you expect me to sell off the family heirlooms?'

'What I expect...' Cecil corrected himself. 'What the queen expects is loyalty from her subjects. That is the only way back into her favour. Keeping company with Catholic renegades like Monteagle will lead to nothing but trouble for you.'

'I consider myself warned,' smiled Essex.

The Beagle scanned the long side wall of the house, muttering to himself. 'He's in there somewhere, I know it.' Then he leaned down from his saddle to speak into the earl's ear. Tom, standing behind the earl, bent ever so slightly closer in order to overhear their exchange.

'This was a Catholic household once, was it not, Devereux?'

'It was,' replied Essex.

'So there is likely to be a priest hole then?'

'I have no idea. But if there is one, I would love to know where it is.'

The Beagle's eyes widened with curiosity. 'Oh? And why is that?'

'Because, my dear Cecil, you never know – I might find Monteagle hiding in there!'

Cecil glowered at him, then kicked his spurs and galloped after his men.

Tom smiled to himself. He enjoyed witnessing his master get the better of the Beagle. Essex beckoned to Sir Gelly, and the two entered into intense, murmured conversation. Tom awaited his orders. He hoped that the household would return to some semblance of normality now, despite the presence of Cecil's eight yeomen-spies in their midst.

Suddenly, his attention was diverted by a sound. He turned to see a pebble bouncing along the cobbles towards him. It came to rest a few inches from his right foot. Wondering who had thrown it, he glanced up, and got a very big surprise.

Chapter 11

The Intruder

Alice could hear the squawk of scavenging pigeons and the cry of the watermen – *Cross the river! Only a shilling! Half a shilling for a sculler!* She could smell the putrid water of the Thames and feel its chill wetness lapping at her shoes. The locket clasped in her hand was pressed tightly to her chest.

'Adam!' cried Edmund.

She raised her head and through tear-starred eyes saw her friend's anxious face looking down at her.

'The tide is coming in,' he said. 'We'd best be heading back.'

'I'll just stay a while longer,' said Alice.

In truth, she really wanted to be alone – alone with Richard. It was hard to explain. But if the river had claimed him, she wanted to be here by the river as it rose. She didn't want to die – didn't think so, anyway – she just wanted to be close to her brother, feel as he might have felt in his final moments as the waters embraced him.

'Sure you won't come back with me?' Edmund asked.

'I'm sure,' she said, and to show him that she wasn't planning on taking her own life, she got to her feet and went over to the steps, climbing a few so she was well above the river. 'You go on now, Edmund,' she said, seating herself there. 'Don't worry about me.'

'Very well, if you're sure…'

Alice listened as his footsteps faded away. When she was certain he was out of sight, she slid down a little way to the dark, slimy steps just above the waterline, so that her shoes were splashed by the wavelets that came rolling in from the wakes of passing boats.

Oh Richard! What shall I do now you've gone?

He'd been her sole companion, her confidant, for as long as she could remember. They'd been through so much together. It had been the two of them against the world, and the bond they'd forged had seemed unbreakable. She found it hard to picture how her life could continue without him. Who would she talk to, argue with, play jokes upon? Who would teach her about history, and how to shoot with a bow and arrow? Who would comfort her when she was sad?

She looked down at the locket, now closed again. What were the odds of finding it here of all places? It was almost as though forces beyond her understanding had conspired to bring it to her so she could know of her brother's fate. What was it Hamlet had said? *There are more things in heaven and earth, Horatio, than are dreamt of in your philosophy.* Maybe he was right.

Alice ran a forefinger against the locket's engraved silver case. This had been their mother's guilt-ridden parting gift before she abandoned them, and Alice had spent much of her life hating it for that very reason. But as she held the ornament, she realised her feelings towards it had changed. This object, which Richard had loved, had by some strange magic found its way back to her, and now she knew she would treasure it to her dying day.

As she sat there studying it, a small frown passed across her features. There was something not quite right about the locket. The case was perfectly dry. She had found it in the damp sand, yet the locket itself had been as dry as a bone when she'd picked it up – almost as if…

She twisted around and peered up towards the top of the steps.

… almost as if it had fallen, or been tossed down, onto the beach from the bank above.

Alice suddenly leapt to her feet and raced up the steps. When she reached the top, she whirled about, looking keenly in all directions. She saw lighters unloading cargo at a nearby wharf, and porters carrying crates into a warehouse. She saw a rich gentleman and his wife haggling with a barge owner over a fare, an oyster seller with her tray, and a juggler tossing colourful balls in the air, entertaining the crowds as they queued up for the bear garden.

It was a perfectly ordinary scene. Who had she hoped to see? Richard? His captor? Whoever had dropped or thrown the locket onto the sand would be long gone by now, and there was no hope now of finding him. Yet this thought did nothing to prevent her rising elation. Only a moment ago she had given up her brother for dead, assuming he'd drowned in the river. Now, she had hope. He hadn't drowned – not for certain, anyway. The search could continue!

Alice placed the chain of the locket around her neck. Then, with a spring in her step, she raced down to the jetty and approached the nearest waterman.

'Where to, young sir?'

'Essex House, if you please,' she said as she leapt aboard his wherry boat.

Twenty minutes later, they docked at a jetty beneath the Essex House watergate. Alice stepped out of the boat. The watergate was an imposing stone monument with an archway in its centre, constructed at the top of a broad flight of steps that rose out of the river. Set within the archway was a pair of tall, wrought-iron gates, closed and bolted from the inside. This did not daunt her. She had faced such obstacles before, during her life as a street urchin after she and Richard ran away from the orphanage. When really hungry, they had occasionally broken into townhouse gardens and stolen cabbages and onions from their vegetable patches and sometimes fruit from their trees. It was often easier to obtain food from such places than from the markets with their eagle-eyed stall-holders.

Those days were well and truly behind her, but Alice had retained the skills of stealth and watchfulness. She could scale a wall quickly and silently, and remain crouched and perfectly still for minutes on end. She waited for the waterman to row away, then moved along to the far end of the steps. Holding on tight to the big cornerstone of the watergate, she stretched out one leg towards a ledge running along the base of a wall set back from the gate – the wall that bordered the garden of Essex House. It was a big stretch, and if her hands slipped she would tumble into the filthy river. Once her foot was resting on the ledge, she carefully edged her body along the side wall of the watergate. It was precarious – her left foot kept slipping off the slimy green stone, and she had to cling on using fingerholds just half an inch deep. But Alice was strong and light and agile, and very soon she'd got herself onto the ledge. The wall above her was low, and its brickwork easily scalable. The top was crenellated in the style of a battlement, as if Essex House was a castle. She scrambled upwards and managed to get her hands into a crenel, or gap, in the battlement, then levered herself up. The garden on the other side was beautiful, and for a moment she could only stare at it. Through the misty air, the trees appeared like tall ghosts with their pale, skin-like bark, and the grass lay on the ground in folds like rich green velvet. It was a little patch of paradise within the great big, dirty city.

Once she'd checked that there was no one around, Alice jumped down from the wall and landed on the soft earth of the garden. She began moving slowly through the trees, keeping well away from the clear area bordering the path. She passed through an ancient sunken courtyard and spied a little bench beneath a sheltering oak where she imagined lovers might meet and dream together. Closer to the house, she came upon a knot garden with low, neatly trimmed hedges grown in maze-like, symmetrical patterns on a gravel bed.

Beyond the knot garden was a brick wall with an impressive arched opening leading to a large central court. If she went through there she would be spotted immediately. Instead, she crept through another, smaller gap in the wall and found herself in a dirty little kitchen yard. There were chickens running about, and a maid was there, emptying slops into a ditch. The maid had her back to Alice, and she was able to dash across the yard and hide behind the well.

When the maid returned to the kitchen, Alice scooted over to an oak door set into a wall at the far end. Pushing the door ajar, she could look out across the central courtyard without being seen. There seemed to be a lot going on. At the far end of the quadrangle, ranks of impressively disciplined men in scarlet uniforms were marching through a gate. Their departure was being watched by other men wearing beards and shabby uniforms who were standing around the edges of the court. Another group dressed like knights or nobles, some of them on horses, were gathered outside the main entrance to the house. Alice wondered if one of them might be Lord Monteagle and how she could possibly find out.

Then she noticed that one of these smartly dressed men was actually a boy – and a boy she recognized! It was Tom, looking quite dashing in his house servant's livery. *He* would be able to tell her where to find Monteagle. But first she needed to attract his attention without anyone else noticing. Fortunately, at that moment, the mounted men suddenly galloped away and several of the other gentlemen returned to the house, leaving just three standing by the entrance, including Tom. The other two became immersed in conversation, so Tom was, for the moment, on his own. This was her chance! Scanning the ground around her she spotted a small pebble. She scooped it up and, taking careful aim, tossed it towards where Tom was standing.

Chapter 12

The Picture Gallery

The pebble landed close to Tom's foot. He looked down, looked up, and saw her. His eyes grew big with shock.

Good! she thought. That meant he'd recognised her – despite her boy outfit. Tom checked to make sure that the other two were still engrossed in their conversation, then sidled away from them. Soon, he picked up speed, walking very quickly towards the doorway where Alice was waiting. After another quick glance over his shoulder, he grabbed her arm and pulled her through the door, shutting it behind them.

'Ophelia?' he gasped. 'Is it really you?'

'Of course it's me!' she said, yanking her arm free of his painfully tight grip. 'And it's Adam, by the way.'

He studied her short hair and sheepskin doublet with a sceptical eye. 'I'm still not entirely convinced you're a boy.'

'I don't care what you think,' she said dismissively.

'Why are you here?'

'To find Monteagle, of course,' she said. 'I wish to ask him about my brother. You *have* to take me to him.'

This demand made Tom grimace. '*Everyone* is after Monteagle today,' he said. 'That man on horseback you just saw leaving – he is chief minister to the queen, the most powerful man in the kingdom, and he's spent all morning searching for him.'

Alice was downcast by this news, but also curious. 'What does the chief minister want with him?'

Tom shrugged. 'He believes him mixed up in some plot or other.'

Alice fingered the scroll in her sleeve. 'The same plot that my brother became mixed up in perhaps.'

'What *is* that scroll?' Tom asked.

'I found it among Richard's possessions,' she said. 'I think it contains a secret code – as well as Monteagle's crest.'

'May I see it?'

She handed it to him, and he looked quizzically at the code in much the same way that Edmund had done. Finally, he shook his head and handed it back.

Alice sighed. 'I suppose this means I've made a wasted journey.'

'How so?'

'Well if the most powerful man in England can't

find Monteagle, then what chance do I have?'

'Every chance!' declared Tom.

'What do you mean?' she asked, heartened by his confident smile.

'I'll show you. But first…'

'What?'

'You're a talented player, aren't you, Adam?'

'No.'

'Well *I* think you are. And now you must play the part of a servant, otherwise I will never get you to where we need to go.'

Some footsteps behind them made them both turn sharply. A maid servant came out into the yard – a thin, red-haired woman, hobbling under the weight of a large bucket, which she was carrying over to the well.

'Amy!' called Tom.

She looked up. 'Aye, Tom?'

'Sir Gelly has recruited a new housemaid…' For this error he got a painful kick in the ankle from Alice. 'I–I mean groom – but he needs some suitable attire. Do you have anything?'

'Aye, I should think so. Try the scullery.'

Tom led Alice into the kitchen and from there into the little room at the back containing large tubs for scrubbing clothing. Tom selected a few items that had been hung out to dry on a wooden frame, and handed them to Alice. They were the typical livery of a groom – the doublet and hose of a young gentleman, though of a more sober, dark blue shade and less fashionable cut.

Alice looked at him, then down at the clothes.

'Well?' said Tom. 'What are you waiting for? Try them on.'

Why was this always happening to her?

She looked around the room. The wooden frame, draped with clothing, offered some privacy, so she moved behind it and started to get changed.

'Shy, aren't you – for a player!' remarked Tom. Alice ignored him.

The clothing was a little on the large side, which suited her, as it hid her curves. When she was ready, Tom led her out of the kitchen and along a corridor to the Great Hall.

It was bigger than the main hall at the orphanage and filled with beautiful objects, from suits of gleaming armour to enormous and intricately woven wall-hangings showing rural scenes of hunting and farming. There was an enormous hearth – almost the size of the rooms at Mrs Fairfax's house. Coloured sunlight streamed through the stained-glass windows making pretty patterns on the stone floor.

Beyond the Great Hall was another impressive room with a grand staircase leading off it. Hearing footsteps, they froze. Tom pulled her behind a pillar. From this hiding place she glimpsed a pair of soldiers in scarlet tunics carrying long, scary-looking weapons over their shoulders. They marched out of a doorway and ascended the stairs. Once they were out of sight, Tom nodded at her, then led her quickly across the room and into a corridor.

'Those are yeomen of the guard – the chief minister's men,' he whispered to her. 'We must avoid them at all costs.'

She followed him along the corridor and then into a long room filled with paintings. He closed the door behind them.

'Why did you bring me here?' asked Alice.

'Ssshh!' hissed Tom. 'Not so loud. Monteagle is very close.'

Alice cast her eyes around the room. 'Has he turned into a painting then?' she asked with a faint smirk.

'No,' murmured Tom, 'but he might be behind one of them.' He wandered over to the large painting at the far end of the room and began examining it.

Alice went and stood alongside him. 'You'd better tell me what's going on,' she said.

'There's a priest hole in this house,' he explained, 'and the entrance is behind one of the paintings in this room. Monteagle is hiding in the priest hole.'

'Do you think he's behind *this* painting then?'

'This painting is called *The Ambassadors* – it contains the clue,' said Tom. 'Somewhere in it is a number between one and thirty. That should tell us which of the thirty paintings has the entrance behind it.'

Alice nodded, understanding at last, and the two of them began hunting for the number. They had imagined it would be a straightforward search for a single number hidden somewhere within the painting. With mounting dismay, they soon realised that the painting was *full* of numbers – there were numerals on both sundials, on the quadrant, on the torquetum (an astronomical instrument) and in the book of arithmetic. It wasn't a case of finding a number – it was a case of *which one*? Alice noted that the book of hymns on the bottom shelf of the cabinet was open at Hymn XIX, or 19. Tom discovered the number '25' inscribed on the dagger belonging to one of the men. Alice found '29' on a book the other man was leaning on.

The other challenge they faced was how to assign numbers to the thirty paintings in the room. Should they be counted from the door or from *The Ambassadors*? And should they be counted off in a clockwise direction or anticlockwise? It was Tom who found the solution to this particular problem when he noticed '15' carved in tiny numerals in the bottom corner of the frame of *The Ambassadors*.

'I think the paintings are numbered,' he said, pointing this out. Alice checked the neighbouring painting on the right, and quickly found the number '16' inscribed in the same place in its frame. That was one issue settled. Now they had to work out which of the painting's many numbers was the one they needed.

They decided to begin with Painting 19 – the number they'd found in the hymnal. It was a portrait of a sombre-looking gentleman with an enormous ruff. Tom was in the act of taking it down when they heard footsteps in the corridor, and the door behind them squeaked open. As quick as he could, Tom replaced the painting on its hook and turned to face whoever was coming into the room.

Two yeomen entered – the same pair they'd seen earlier.

'Why are you in here?' one of them barked.

Alice saw Tom's flushed cheeks. His mouth opened but no words emerged, and she knew she would have to come up with something herself, and fast.

Chapter 13

A Fresh Angle

'We're carrying out a painting inspection,' Alice announced.

Tom turned and stared at her, mouth still agape.

'What do you mean?' demanded the yeoman.

'S-Sir Gelly's orders,' stammered Tom. 'Once a month, we must inspect the paintings, to see if – if…'

'If any are missing,' said Alice.

'Or replaced,' added Tom.

'Or damaged,' Alice put in for good measure.

The yeomen did not look entirely convinced by this story.

'We will go now and verify what you say with Sir Gelly,' said the other one. 'What are your names?'

'Tom,' said Tom, 'and um…'

'Adam,' said Alice.

'We shall return anon,' the first yeoman said, and they left.

Tom sank against the wall, closing his eyes. 'We're done for,' he sighed. 'There's no such thing as a painting inspection, nor any groom employed here called Adam. Those guards will be back at any moment once they've spoken with Sir Gelly. They'll assume we're in league with Monteagle, and we'll surely be hanged for treason.' He frowned at her.

'Why am I even doing this?'

She shrugged. 'Because you want to help me find my brother?'

'I'm a fool,' grimaced Tom, half to himself. 'I had a good position here and I've thrown it all away.' He turned to her, a feverish glint in his eyes. 'Maybe we should escape now while we can.'

Alice bit her lip, feeling guilty for the danger she was placing him in – yet she couldn't just give up. She touched the locket on her chest. 'I'm not going anywhere until I've spoken to Monteagle,' she decided. 'You can leave if you want to, but I have to find that priest hole.'

Without waiting for Tom to object, she reached up and lifted Painting 19 off its hook. There was no sign of an entry point in the oak-panelled wall behind it – not even the finest line or groove in the wood that might indicate the presence of a hidden door. Determined not to show her disappointment, she rehung it and strode over to Painting 25. Again, she found nothing unusual behind it. The wall behind Painting 29 was equally blank.

'It's useless,' said Tom. 'There are too many numbers in *The Ambassadors*, and we don't have time to check behind every painting.'

Alice went back to *The Ambassadors*. 'There's something simple that we're missing,' she said, scanning the canvas once again.

'There's nothing simple about that pai...'

Tom didn't get any further. Hearing a sliding sound behind her, Alice spun around to see what had happened.

She found him sprawled on the floor, nursing a sore knee.

'Why are you down there?' she almost laughed.

'Tripped on something,' said Tom, picking up the strange-looking object that had up-ended him. He gazed at it wonderingly. 'It looks like it fell right out of that painting.'

Alice had to agree – it was a brass instrument very similar in style to the devices depicted on the upper shelf of the cabinet in *The Ambassadors*. The instrument resembled an elongated capital G. The curved part of the G was inscribed at its edge with tiny numbers. Attached to the vertical line of the G was a rod that could be swivelled around the arc of the curve to point to the numbers.

Tom traced a finger around the curve of the instrument. 'I wonder what it does?'

'I think it measures things,' said Alice. She took

it from him and moved the pivoted rod to different points along the curve. 'See?'

Tom scrambled to his feet, suddenly excited. 'Angles,' he said. 'It measures angles.'

'Angles?' frowned Alice. Vaguely she remembered Richard, who often had his head in a book, telling her about Angles and Saxons. He said they were ancient peoples of England. She wondered why anyone would want to measure them.

'Sir Gelly, the steward, took Monteagle here earlier to find the priest hole,' Tom was muttering. 'Perhaps he did so using this. That must be why it's here. So then the number we want refers to an angle.'

'Of course,' said Alice, still not understanding him but too embarrassed to admit her ignorance. She watched as Tom started placing the instrument against different parts of the painting, lining it up against objects, swivelling the pivoted rod and reading off the numbers. Not for the first time, she rued her lack of education.

Tom kept up a running commentary as he shifted around the painting. 'The angle between the edges of the hymn book's covers is 27 degrees,' he said. 'The angle between the lute and the carpenter's square is 27 degrees.... The angle between the skull and the floor is... 27 degrees.'

The number 27 kept coming up, and this sparked a memory in Alice. She had seen that number elsewhere in the painting. It didn't take her long to find it again: 27 was painted on the quadrant. She also found it on the polyhedral sundial, and on the torquetum. The more she looked, the more instances she found of the number 27.

After a short while, they stopped looking at the painting and turned and faced each other. Then, without a word passing between them, they both raced over to Painting 27, which was towards the far end of the room near the door. The painting showed a noblewoman in a red dress with gold embroidery and long, loose sleeves. Tom quickly took it down and they both anxiously examined the wall behind.

Nothing was there but plain oak panelling – exactly the same as behind all the other paintings. Alice felt herself start to despair.

Just as they were absorbing this latest disappointment, they heard footsteps approaching urgently along the corridor outside.

'The yeomen are back already!' groaned Tom, looking sick with despair.

The door opened, and a groom entered. Tom let out a relieved breath. 'Owen,' he said.

'Sir Gelly's looking for you,' said Owen, with a bemused glance at Alice. 'He wants to know where you disappeared to.'

'Tell him you can't find me,' said Tom.

'What?'

'I'll explain it all later!'

Alice could tell that Owen wasn't satisfied with this. 'We've been given a secret assignment,' she told him.

'Why doesn't Sir Gelly know about it?' asked Owen.

'Because it's too secret even for Sir Gelly,' Alice improvised. 'We're under orders from the earl himself, and if you don't leave us in peace, the earl will hear of it.'

'Enough said!' muttered Owen as he began backing out of the room.

Just when they thought he had gone, he came back in. 'It's mad today, mad I tell you!' he whined. 'We've got the redcoats poking their noses everywhere, and now it's secret assignments! I'm just trying to do my job...' He glanced out into the corridor, and uttered an oath. 'Two more of those blasted yeomen heading this way.' With that, he ducked out of the room and was gone.

'Now we really are done for!' gasped Tom.

Alice didn't reply. She was crouching near the floor, staring at the panelling just below Painting 27. 'See that line?' she murmured, pointing to a barely visible seam between the left-hand edge of one of the rectangular recessed panels and its frame.

Tom paled when he saw this. He slammed his fist into his palm.

'What's wrong?' cried Alice.

'Sir Gelly said *beneath*. He said the entrance was *beneath* the painting. I thought he meant *behind* it! That must be the door. Push it!'

Alice pushed at it, but it didn't budge.

'Open!' she screamed at the wall.

They both heard the familiar echoing sound of footsteps approaching along the corridor. Alice pushed frantically at the panel to no effect, as the footsteps came steadily closer.

'There's something over here,' said Tom.

Alice looked up to see him poking at something on the right-hand side of the neighbouring panel. It was tiny, and could have been a splinter or minor imperfection in the wood – but looking closer, she saw that it was a miniature latch. Tom swivelled it to the open position, and the other panel, which Alice was still leaning on, suddenly swung inwards, causing Tom's panel to sweep outwards, almost hitting him in the face. For a second, they both stared in shock at what they'd discovered: a revolving door with a central shaft hidden within the frame between the two panels.

Then they heard the squeak of the door handle behind them starting to turn. Alice pushed herself through the little doorway – which was no more than twelve inches in height – into the dark space beyond. Tom wriggled after her and kicked the double-panel door shut behind him. They lay there in the darkness, breathing hard and listening as boots squeaked across the parquet floor, coming ever closer to Painting 27. Had the yeomen seen the little door close?

Chapter 14

The Priest Hole

The footsteps, distinctly audible through the thin wooden panelling, reached a crescendo of volume. Then, to Alice's immense relief, they gradually grew fainter. Eventually, she heard the click of the door closing.

By this time, her eyes had become adapted to the darkness, which was not complete thanks to a thin, gauzy light filtering in through a small iron grille a few yards from where they lay. They were in a narrow, very low-ceilinged passage running parallel with the room they had just left. One wall was formed of the rear of the oak panelling; the other, of dark, dusty bricks.

Standing was impossible, with a wooden ceiling positioned just a few feet above their prone bodies. So, with Alice taking the lead, they began crawling along the passage, heading towards the far end, near to where *The Ambassadors* was hung. The further they went, the gloomier it became, and Alice was soon obliged to feel her way with her hands. Every yard or so, she would stop to brush her fingers against the brick wall on her right, trying to locate the entrance to the priest hole. Eventually, she found what felt like the edge of a little wooden door set within the brickwork. She was about to push the door open when Tom grabbed her wrist.

'Wait!' he breathed.

At the same moment, the passage brightened as outside light flooded in, and from behind them there came a frenzied scuffling, which sounded to Alice like a large sack being squeezed through a hole too small for its bulk. She froze, skin tingling.

Someone else must be coming! Had they been seen?

Alice twisted around and peered past Tom to witness a large figure pushing its way in through the same secret door that they had just come through. Hastily, she and Tom slithered further up the passage, past the wooden door, to the far end where the darkness was absolute. There they crouched, eyes wide, senses alert, like rats in the skirting board, waiting to see who was coming their way. As the figure loomed closer, Tom flinched. 'It's Sir Gelly, the steward,' he said under his breath. Sir Gelly groped blindly towards them, his face plump and glistening with sweat. If he saw them now, they would be utterly trapped. To their great relief, he didn't spot them. His hand fumbled for the little wooden door on the right, he pushed it ajar and squeezed inside.

Alice had just begun breathing again when she spotted more movement at the far end of the passageway.

'There's someone else,' whispered Tom.

They watched and waited as a second figure made its way slowly towards them. It was another man, even bigger than Sir Gelly. He had ruddy cheeks and a bushy beard. As he came into view, Alice started to tremble. She clapped her hand over her mouth to prevent herself from crying out.

The man who was now edging his bulk through the little wooden door was none other than Gus Phillips. Only the day before he had been treading the boards as Polonius in Hamlet! *What was he doing here?*

'Wasn't that the fellow who I thought was murdered on stage yesterday?' gasped Tom as soon as the door had swung shut.

'Aye, that was Gus,' confirmed a slightly dizzy Alice. 'Why would *he* be meeting with Lord Monteagle?'

Tom shrugged, equally bewildered. 'Let's see if we can find out.'

They crept closer to the small door and tried to hear what was being said, but the voices were muffled and indistinct and they only managed to catch tiny snatches of the conversation. Lord Monteagle and Sir Gelly seemed to be doing most of the talking. Their tone was alternately charming and forceful, occasionally verging on pleading. Among the phrases that Alice managed to make out from the general burble of voices were: 'a special performance', 'King Richard II' and 'the banned scene'.

As Alice listened, a chill of understanding began to steal over her. Just before he disappeared, Richard had warned her that plots were being hatched and that people weren't all they seemed. He must have been talking about Gus! Gus had become involved in some plot with Monteagle and the steward, and then lured Richard to join them, probably with promises of money or promotion to hired-man status. It was Gus's fault that Richard had disappeared.

Anger and a desperate desire to know what had happened to her brother made her want to break through the door. Her muscles flexed. 'I'm going in there,' she whispered between clenched teeth. 'I'm going to force them to tell me everything!'

'No!' Tom breathed, and she felt his hand on her elbow, pulling her back from the door.

She took a deep breath, trying to regain control of her emotions.

'What's wrong with you?' Tom asked.

She told him about Richard's warning to her, and her realisation that he had been talking about Gus. 'Those men in there, they know what's happened to him. I have to make them tell me!'

She was becoming worked up again, and would have pushed her way through the door if Tom hadn't maintained his vicelike grip on her.

'If we go in there now, they might kill us,' he hissed. 'Sir Gelly's a former soldier and he always carries a knife. It won't help your brother if we end up dead in this rat-hole.'

She stopped struggling. It wasn't that she cared so much about the danger to herself, she just realised that it wasn't fair on Tom – she had no right to risk the life of someone who was helping her.

'We need to gather more evidence,' Tom told her. 'We need to find out what this plot is all about. You never know, we might be able to discover where your brother is without getting killed in the process.'

'How are we going to do that?' Alice sighed.

'I have an idea,' he told her. 'Let's get out of here and I'll explain.'

Reluctantly, she followed him back down the passageway, through the disguised door and into the picture gallery. Tom crossed the room and opened one of the mullioned windows. After motioning Alice to follow, he clambered through it. With a graceful leap, she followed him out, landing next to him in some rose bushes. From there, it was a short walk back through the garden to the wall by the river.

'So, what's your master plan?' she asked him when they had arrived there.

'The code on that paper of yours,' said Tom, indicating the little scroll peeping out from the hem of her sleeve. 'I know someone who's an expert on that sort of thing. Perhaps he can help us break it.'

'Truly?' She was surprised and pleased to hear this, and her smile, she noticed, greatly cheered him.

I should try to be more appreciative, she told herself.

'We can go there now, if you wish,' he said.

Alice shook her head. 'You have done more than enough for me, Tom, risking the wrath of your steward and your position in this house, and all to help someone you barely know. If you tell me where I can find this code-breaking gentleman, I will go to him myself.'

Tom hesitated. She saw conflicting emotions flicker briefly in his face, as if he were waging a private battle with himself. Several times he glanced back towards the house before finally coming to a decision. 'I will go with you,' he said. 'It's not only for your sake. I promised this man – his name is Sir Francis Bacon – that I would keep him informed about… about events at Essex House. This plot involving your brother has, I fear, far-reaching consequences. I think it is my duty to inform Sir Francis about what we have discovered.'

Alice nodded, her guilt about involving Tom somewhat assuaged. She wasn't, if truth be told, unhappy to be accompanied by this young man. He had proved himself intelligent and intuitive in their efforts to locate the priest hole. Also, she had to concede, perhaps his instincts had not been so entirely off the mark in dissuading her from confronting Gus, Monteagle and the steward in their little den. All in all, she could probably do a lot worse than have him along.

After checking no one was watching, they climbed over the wall and inched their way around the watergate to the jetty. 'No one will notice this gone for an hour or so,' said Tom, stepping aboard one of the three barges moored there. Alice took a seat by one of the oars, and Tom slid in next to her after he had unhitched the mooring rope. Then the two of them began to ease the barge into the river.

Chapter 15

York House

They rowed with a steady rhythm upstream towards Sir Francis Bacon's residence at York House. To their right, on the north bank of the river, lay the former bishop's palaces, now owned by wealthy courtiers, their red-tiled rooftops and fluttering flags visible above the walls and ornamental watergates. To their left lay the fields and farms of Lambeth Marshes.

It was cold on the river. The chill breeze cut like steel through the fine fabric of their servant's livery, and Tom wished that he'd had the presence of mind to help himself to a couple of woollen cloaks before they'd set out. Not for the first time today, he wondered why he was prepared to endure such discomfort and take such risks for the sake of someone he barely knew.

If he was honest with himself, he knew the reason, but it still didn't make any sense. The reason, he supposed, was that the beautiful Ophelia had cast a spell over him. It didn't matter how many times he told himself that Ophelia did not exist – that she was actually a boy named Adam – it made no difference to his feelings. When he had first set eyes on Adam this morning, standing there at the entrance to the kitchen yard, what he actually had seen was Ophelia dressed up as a boy – a reversal of yesterday's experience at the Globe. Adam had, of course, insisted that he was a boy, and common sense supported his claim – for Tom knew that no girl could ever be a player. Even so, he could not deny what he had seen, and ever since that moment it had been Ophelia that Tom had wanted to help.

Yet here was the strange thing: the longer Tom spent in Adam's company, the less the question of his gender actually mattered. Whether boy or girl, he retained the same mysterious, melancholy, magical presence that had captured and held Tom's attention as he'd stood there in the yard of the Globe. And he could scarcely believe that the same person who had lit up the stage yesterday was now seated here next to him in this barge. Today, he had risked his life and his position for Adam with scarcely a second thought. Sir Gelly may have already decided to dismiss him – yet he felt no regret. He would do it all again, and more, for Adam.

Their oars cleaved the pale green silk of the river in steady beats. The breeze chilled the sweat on Tom's brow to ice-water. The low, silver-grey clouds seemed to press down on him with an air of implacable menace. His world was changing, and it wasn't only because of the arrival of Adam. There was intrigue and skulduggery at Essex House – whispers of plots. Of course he felt compassion for his master's distress, and anger at the way he had been treated by his enemies at court, yet he feared what he might be planning. Did the earl actually think he could take on Robert Cecil and beat him?

'Do you have any family?' Adam suddenly asked him, breaking into these dark thoughts.

'The folk at Essex House are my family,' he replied.

'*Real* family, I mean.'

'My parents died when I was six, during the plague outbreak of '93.' Tom said this matter-of-factly, as if speaking about another boy's life. It was how he liked to think of it – as another boy's life. Better that than risk exposing himself to the real, raw memories of that time.

'That must have been horrible,' said Adam. 'What happened after that? Where did you live?'

'I went to live with my uncle. He was rich, but cruel. He instructed me in manners, taught me how to be a gentleman, and beat me when I made mistakes. But I learned enough to be taken into service as a groom at Essex House.'

'You're an orphan then, like me,' said Adam,

smiling. Tom smiled back, and for a brief moment he no longer felt the cold.

York House came into view on the north bank. It was an impressive sight with its square, crenellated turrets and the spire rising from its central roof. Tom pointed it out to Adam, and they began steering the barge towards its watergate.

As they neared the jetty, Tom felt a sudden twinge of doubt. He had come here because he wished to protect his master from the enemies who would destroy him, and the 'friends', like Monteagle, who would lead him to destruction. The one man he could trust in this dangerous predicament was Sir Francis Bacon. So why did this feel so much like betrayal?

They edged the nose of their barge between a couple of other boats on the jetty. Tom was first out and he tethered the barge to a mooring post. Then the two of them ascended the steps and rang the iron bell on the watergate.

Soon, a porter appeared on the other side of the gate. He studied them dubiously. 'Do you have a message?' he asked.

'We have come to see your master on urgent business,' said Tom. 'We are grooms at Essex House.'

'Your names?'

'I am Tom Cavendish, and this is Adam, er…'

'Fletcher,' finished Adam.

'The master isn't at home,' said the porter bluntly.

Tom sighed with disappointment – but he also felt a strange sort of relief.

'When will he return?' asked Adam.

'I know not. He is at court and keeps irregular hours. He may decide to dine in the City this evening. You may leave a message, if you wish.'

'Please tell Sir Francis that Tom Cavendish has information for him,' said Tom.

'We shall wait for him,' said Adam.

Tom looked at Adam in surprise. He cut a slight figure in his baggy, oversized servant's livery – yet he stood there, defiant, in the shadow of the enormous arch of the watergate, and Tom couldn't help but feel a swell of admiration in his chest. *He doesn't give up easily!*

'No you will not,' said the porter. 'You will leave this instant.'

'What ho! Is that young Tom?' cried a voice from the river.

Tom spun around, and nearly fell into the water in surprise. Standing on the curved prow of a luxury barge speeding towards him was Sir Francis Bacon. The barge, propelled by four powerfully built oarsmen, slid into a vacant berth, and Sir Francis vaulted smoothly onto the jetty.

'What a pleasure to see you, my friend!' said Sir Francis, running up the steps and clapping an arm around his shoulder. 'Have you been keeping your eyes open for me as I asked?'

'Aye, sir,' answered Tom, and when he saw the little philosopher's merry, twinkling smile, he knew that he had made the right decision in coming here.

'Good man! Good man! You have information for me then, I take it?'

'I have, sir.'

'Excellent! ... And who pray is this?'

Sir Francis had come to a sudden halt in front of Adam.

'I am Adam Fletcher, sire,' said Adam, with a bend of the knee and a bow of the head. 'I work with Tom at Essex House. I am most honoured to meet you.'

'Welcome, Adam,' said Sir Francis. 'Please, both of you, step this way...'

The porter had, by now, opened the gate, and Sir Francis led them through the garden to the house. It was a large, classically designed garden, with neat gravel paths and lines of bushes laid out in geometric patterns. Despite his smallness of stature, Sir Francis could move very quickly, and Tom and Adam almost had to trot to keep up with him as they followed him through a large inner courtyard and into the house. Tom was impressed by the size of the great hall – its enormous, intricate hammerbeam roof reminded him of the interior of a ship's hull. Yet he was surprised to see so few paintings or tapestries displayed on the walls. There weren't any suits of armour, weapons or shields either. Everything was grander in scale and at the same time less showy than at Essex House.

The most impressive room by far was the library. They gasped at its size, and at the thousands of books lining the shelves that stretched from the floor to the ceiling. This, truly, was a cathedral of learning.

And it did not only contain books. On display tables dotted about the room were mysterious and intricate mechanical instruments that would not have looked out of place in the *Ambassadors* painting. While the Earl of Essex loved art and the glamour of war, Tom realized that Sir Francis was far more interested in scholarship and natural philosophy.

He introduced them to a few of the instruments, as they both seemed so intrigued. Pointing to a globe made up of brass hoops and spheres, he explained it was an *orrery*, a mechanical model of the solar system, which predicted the motions of the moon and planets. He showed them a disc with a sinuous, maze-like pattern of lines on its surface, which he called an *astrolabe*, a device used for astronomy and navigation. There were other machines there that delighted their eyes and minds: a miniature windmill and an astronomical clock with its weights and gears exposed.

But the object Sir Francis seemed most excited by was perhaps the least interesting visually. It was a narrow tube of brass, around ten inches in length, with circular pieces of glass inserted into both ends. He offered it to Tom. 'Look through this,' he said.

Tom peered through one end of the tube, and was surprised to see that the books on Sir Francis's shelves appeared much closer. He could almost read the titles on their spines.

'It's extraordinary!' he cried, now turning the tube on Adam. His eyelashes were clearly delineated, as were the fine details of his lips, nose, cheeks and hair. Tom lingered on this view. He felt as though he could reach out and touch him.

At length, he handed the object back to Sir Francis, who pointed out the glass at the far end of the tube. 'Notice how it is curved like the lenses in a pair of eyeglasses,' he said. 'When the light passes through it, the curved glass bends it. The two lenses work together to focus the light and make everything appear much closer… And this is just the beginning. I predict that one day we will be able to make these seeing-tubes so powerful that they will reveal to us the secrets of the very small, and…' – he pointed out of the window at the sky – '…of the very far away.

'We live in an exciting age,' he told them. 'New discoveries are being made all the time. For centuries, mankind has been sleeping. We have relied on ancient books for answers to the riddles of existence. Yet we can learn so much more simply by the use of our senses, with the aid of instruments like this one. Everything depends on keeping the eye steadily fixed upon the *facts* of nature, so that we see things as they are, and not as we imagine them to be.'

Every moment spent in Sir Francis's company seemed to expand Tom's idea of what being alive could mean. It didn't only have to be about serving wine to your master's guests or fetching wood for the fire. Sir Francis, with his ideas, could light fires in people's minds. Yet, with regret, Tom acknowledged that the pursuit of natural philosophy was not a path open to the likes of him. One had to have leisure and money, and Tom would never have either of those. Still, he felt lucky, at least, to be able to stand here in this room and listen and learn from a man like Sir Francis Bacon.

Chapter 16

Examining the Evidence

'And speaking of keeping our eyes open,' said Sir Francis, 'you said you had some news for me, Tom.'

Tom glanced at Adam. 'Aye, sir. We, that is Adam and I, witnessed a secret meeting today between Sir Gelly Meyrick, Lord Monteagle and, er…' He faltered.

'And another man, Mr Augustus Phillips, who we believe is a player with the Chamberlain's Men,' Adam finished for him.

Sir Francis's eyebrows shot up. 'The Chamberlain's Men – they're the fellows at the Globe, aren't they? The ones who Shakespeare writes plays for. Why would Sir Gelly and Lord Monteagle want to have dealings with one of them?'

'We were surprised, too, sir,' said Tom.

'And what was said at this meeting?'

'We didn't hear much,' admitted Tom. 'We were...'

'You were eavesdropping, weren't you?' chuckled Sir Francis. 'Don't worry, my boy, some of the most significant intelligence in history has come from listening at keyholes. So come on. Out with it! What exactly *did* you hear?'

'We heard them talk of a *special performance,*' said Tom.

'They mentioned *King Richard II,* which is a play by Shakespeare...' added Adam.

'I know the play,' said Sir Francis.

'We also heard the words *banned scene,*' said Tom.

Sir Francis stroked his beard. 'The banned scene from *King Richard II,*' he mused. 'That would be the scene in which the king is deposed – it recreates the moment in 1399 when Henry of Bolingbroke overthrew Richard and crowned himself King Henry IV. That scene is never included in performances of the play, for one simple reason: the queen hates any references to a monarch being forcibly removed from the throne. She fears it may put ideas in people's heads! Do either of you know the sad story of the historian, Dr John Hayward?' He looked at each of them in turn. 'I take it from your blank faces that you do not. Well, let me enlighten you... A couple of years ago, Dr Hayward wrote a history of King Henry IV in which he described how Henry seized the throne from Richard II. Unfortunately, Hayward decided to dedicate his book to your master, the Earl of Essex. This was at a time when Essex was at the height of his popularity in the country, before his disastrous expedition to Ireland. Back then, many people were hoping that he might become our next monarch.

'Well, when this book came to the attention of the queen, she was furious. Hayward, she believed, saw Essex as a modern Henry of Bolingbroke. She thought the book a deliberate attempt to encourage Essex and his followers to overthrow her. The queen ordered me to search through the book to find anything in there that might be considered treasonous, so that she could execute the historian.

'After reading the book from cover to cover, I reported back to her: "Your Majesty, as far as treason is concerned, I can find nothing in this book to warrant chopping off Dr Hayward's head. As to plagiarism, however, I would happily wield the axe myself." I then explained to her that many of the good doctor's sentences were stolen from Tacitus. Luckily for Hayward, plagiarism is not a capital crime. Even so, the queen insisted that he be imprisoned in the Tower, and there he remains to this day – a cruel fate for a historian, even a bad one! Yet what this story shows is that the dethroning of King Richard II, though it happened two hundred years ago, remains an extremely sensitive subject – and one that rather intriguingly connects with both your master the Earl of Essex and the Chamberlain's Men.'

'Do you suppose then, sir,' said Tom, 'that Sir Gelly and Lord Monteagle wish the Chamberlain's Men to perform this play, with the dethronement scene included?'

Sir Francis nodded. 'That would seem to be the case. The question is *why*!'

Tom pondered this, and the only conclusion that presented itself to him was so alarming he dared not say it.

'Well, boy?' said Sir Francis. 'I know you have a theory, so speak!'

Tom was conscious of both Adam and Sir Francis staring at him, so he forced himself to utter the words in his head. 'They're putting on this play, sir, to put in people's heads the idea that a monarch can be overthrown...'

'Which means...' coaxed Sir Francis.

'Which means that they're planning to overthrow... Queen Elizabeth.'

Sir Francis did not react to this in the way Tom had expected. He wasn't shocked or furious – he merely nodded and continued to stroke his beard. 'Aye,' he said. 'That is precisely the conclusion that I myself reached. Like you, I can think of no other reason for putting on this play, banned scene included, than to incite the masses in a rebellion against the queen.'

Sir Francis's words echoed around the room like cannon fire across a battlefield, and Tom was dazed by them. Were Sir Gelly and Monteagle really planning to depose the queen? He had assumed that toppling the chief minister had been the limit of their ambitions. A full-scale rebellion against the queen and her government was a wholly different matter. If it succeeded, Tom could end up as groom to the next king of England. If it failed, he would most likely be hanged along with all the rebels…

'There is something else, sir,' he heard Adam say. Tom turned to see him pull the little scroll from his sleeve and show it to Sir Francis.

'What is this?' asked the philosopher.

'Before I tell you, sir, it is time I was honest about my own situation,' said Adam. 'I am not a groom at Essex House.'

'I thought not,' said Sir Francis with an amused grin. 'I have a good memory for faces and do not recall seeing yours on any previous visit there.'

Adam blushed. 'Sir, I confess am a player with the Chamberlain's Men.'

This made Sir Francis look up. 'Is that so? That is most interesting, for it places you at the very heart of the case we are presently wrestling with.'

Adam looked surprised. 'You do not despise me, then, for my chosen profession?'

'Dear boy, I make it a rule never to despise anyone, especially not a player – unless he is a very bad one, and for that I consider him worse than a thief, for having stolen not only my money, but also my time.'

'He is an extremely *good* player, sir,' declared Tom.

'I do not doubt it, for he is one of the Chamberlain's Men, and I have never seen a bad performance at the

Globe….' Sir Francis spoke these words with only a quarter of his mind on what he was saying, for the focus of his attention was by now firmly upon the scroll: 'What is this document, Adam?' he asked.

'I found it among the possessions of my brother Richard – he disappeared a few days ago. I thought it might offer a clue to what happened to him. Tom told me that the symbol there is Lord Monteagle's family crest…'

'Indeed,' muttered Sir Francis.

'Which leads me to wonder whether Richard became mixed up in the plot involving Mr Phillips, Lord Monteagle and Sir Gelly. The rest is, we thought, a secret code, and Tom suggested that you might be able to help us translate it.'

For several minutes Sir Francis stood in silence gazing at the document, and Tom began to nurture the hope that he would indeed be able to decipher the code for them right there and then.

Eventually, however, he shook his head, clearly baffled. 'Could you leave this with me, Adam? I would like to work on it when I have more time.'

'I am sorry, sir,' replied the boy. 'I have vowed never to let it out of my sight until I have found my brother.'

'I understand your concern,' said Sir Francis. 'But it leaves us with a problem, for I cannot help you unless you give me time to study this document in more depth. Would you allow me to furnish you with a copy while I keep hold of the original? I will of course return it as soon as I have concluded my analysis.'

Adam seemed about to refuse, but finally relented with a nod. 'Please assure me that you will take the utmost care of it, sir.'

'Of course,' said Sir Francis, and he took up a quill from his desk. He dipped it in ink and began to transcribe the letters of the code onto a piece of parchment. Once he'd written them all out, he copied the drawings below it: the horse and carriage with the zig-zag line, and Monteagle's coat of arms.

After handing this to Adam, Sir Francis said: 'My young friends, I want to thank you for bringing all this to my attention. It seems that you may have uncovered something quite significant – possibly a plot against Her Majesty's government, though we don't yet know that for certain. More evidence is needed, and perhaps this secret message, if I can decode it, will provide us with that evidence, as well as information about the fate of your brother, Adam. Rest assured, I shall work on it.... Now, I must bid you farewell, for I have guests arriving in an hour or so and I need to prepare. Charles, my footman, will see you out.'

He pulled a cord that dangled above his desk. The cord trailed up the wall, along the ceiling and disappeared out of the room, and Tom heard a distant bell ring somewhere in the house.

Act Three

4th ~ 6th February 1601

Chapter 17

Adam or Eve

Alice struggled in rehearsals the following morning. She had not made a very good job of learning her lines for her part as Mistress Bridget in *Every Man In His Humour*, and this caused Gus to lose his patience with her.

'What were you doing all yesterday afternoon?' he asked her after she had fluffed her lines for the fourth time in a row.

'I'm sorry, Mr Phillips,' she said. 'I've almost got the words straight now. Next time will be better, I promise.'

'It had better be. We do not want you relying on the Book-Holder this afternoon.' The Book-Holder was the man who stood backstage with a copy of the playbook and prompted players who forgot their lines.

It was a point of pride with the Chamberlain's Men that they very rarely made use of him.

The other players regarded Alice with a mixture of contempt and disappointment. The only sympathetic smile she received was from Edmund. She had yet to find a moment to tell him what had happened to her yesterday after he had left her by the river – no doubt he assumed it had been grief over Richard's death that had caused her to forget her lines.

It was true that Alice's mind had been in turmoil following her visits to Essex and York House, but her uppermost emotions had been anger and frustration – so much so that she had found it impossible to concentrate on anything, least of all learning her lines. Seeing Gus this morning only made matters worse, because whenever she looked at him all she could see was his portly figure squeezing itself along the secret passageway behind the Picture Gallery.

Gus was the cause of Richard's disappearance. Of that, Alice was in no doubt. The question was, what should she do about it? If she confronted him openly, he would most likely deny it. Worse, it could prompt him to destroy all evidence of his actions, and possibly take action against *her*. Alice's only option, therefore, was to use guile.

Gus had a small office in one of the back rooms at the Globe. Here he kept the company's accounts and carried out many of the other administrative tasks involved in running a playhouse. As soon as her part in the rehearsals was over, Alice hastened to this office. Luckily, there was no lock on the door. The only lockable doors in the Globe were those leading to the Props Room, where the props, playbooks and admission receipts were stored; and Wardrobe, which contained the company's most valuable assets – its costumes.

Gus's office was a mess. There were heaps of yellowing documents crowding his desk, along with ink pots, used quills, a leather wineskin, a tray of pipe ash and a fox skull used as a paperweight. Alice wasn't certain what she was looking for, but trusted that she would know it when she found it. Searching through the mounds of paper, she found old playbills and roles, correspondence with local printers, paper merchants, cloth merchants and carpenters, contracts with other sharers and letters from the Master of Revels, the official censor, giving permission for plays to be performed. It was all very normal stuff – exactly the kinds of document one would expect to find in such an office. Alice became ever more fretful as she searched deeper into the pile, aware that time was moving on and Gus might be back at any moment. Yet she could find nothing that hinted at any skulduggery or secret plots – nothing, needless to say, about Richard – and the deeper she dug, the older and yellower the documents became.

'Can I help you with something, Adam?'

The deep voice emanating from the doorway behind her was unmistakeable, and it turned Alice's stomach into a ball of ice.

Gus!

Slowly, miserably, she turned.

Gus was looking disturbingly calm, almost as if he'd expected to find her there.

She stuttered an apology.

'Was there something you were looking for, in particular?' he asked with mock-helpfulness. 'Perhaps I can assist you in finding it.'

His manner was setting her teeth on edge, and shame began to turn to anger. 'I am trying to find out what you've done with my brother!' she blurted.

'Your brother?' frowned Gus. 'Is that what this is all about then?'

'Of course it is,' she said. 'You sent him somewhere, didn't you?'

'What makes you think that?'

Should she show him the scroll? *No!* He would find any excuse to destroy it. *What then?* What justification could she give for her accusation?

'What makes you think that, Adam?' Gus repeated.

When she failed to reply, he frowned. 'Catching you here now, poking your nose into this company's confidential affairs – I could throw you out of the Chamberlain's Men for far less. The other sharers would not oppose me. If you care to remain a prentice with us, you should tell me right now why you believe I had something to do with Richard's disappearance.'

'I–I don't know,' she stammered. 'I just thought maybe… that you sent him somewhere.'

'Where would I send him?'

Alice shrugged helplessly. She had nothing, she realized – just a crest on a piece of paper, a vague connection with Lord Monteagle. If she tried to accuse him of kidnapping Richard on the basis of such flimsy evidence, he would laugh at her.

Gus smiled, and it seemed to Alice a smug smile, one that said: *you have nothing that can hurt me!*

'I have no idea where your brother is,' said Gus. 'But my hunch is that he panicked when asked to play Ophelia, and ran away. He will reappear at some stage. Of that I have little doubt. But Richard does not interest me. *You* interest me, Adam.' Gus came further into the room, his large body surprisingly agile as he picked his way through the mess that lay between them. Soon he was towering over her. '*You* interest me a great deal.'

'I, Mr Phillips?' said Alice, cowering beneath him.

'I know your secret,' said Gus.

'My… secret?'

'Aye!' he grinned. 'You know what I am referring to, don't you, Adam? Or should I call you… *Eve*?'

Alice felt a scream starting up deep inside her. This was the moment she had been dreading for almost two years.

'What are you talking about?' she murmured.

She remembered his words to her the day before – *You were uncommonly convincing as a maid yesterday!* – and that smirk on his face as he'd said it. It was her fault

– she should have refused to play Ophelia. As soon as she'd put on that wig and frock, the game was up.

'I'd guessed the truth before you played Ophelia,' said Gus, as if reading her thoughts. 'I knew you were a girl.'

'It's not true,' she said dully, aware of how unconvincing she sounded.

'You don't have to pretend any more,' said Gus. 'Not with me, anyway. And don't worry: so long as you're cooperative, I won't tell anyone.'

She jerked her head up at this. *Did he mean it?*

'It's a risk,' he admitted. 'If the authorities find out, they could close us down. But I'm prepared to take that chance because I spy an opportunity here. I spy an opportunity for you to help me.'

'Help you?' *What did he mean?*

'I need your assistance with a sensitive matter. If you do this for me, then I promise I won't tell anyone your secret.'

'What would you like me to do?' she asked, realising that by saying this she had tacitly conceded that she was, indeed, a girl.

'We're putting on a performance of Shakespeare's *King Richard II* on Saturday.'

Alice flinched very slightly when she heard this. So they'd guessed right. There really was to be a special performance of this play – almost certainly the first act in a rebellion against the government. Preoccupied as she was with the fate of her brother, she had given little thought to this aspect of the plot they had uncovered. Now she was wondering how Gus was thinking of involving her.

'There's a scene in the play where King Richard is dethroned,' said Gus. 'We've not included that scene since the play was first performed back in 1595. For this performance, I have decided that we should put the scene back in.'

You mean Monteagle has decided, thought Alice.

'We need the author to hand over the scene,' said Gus. 'But the author won't want to.'

'Why is that?'

Gus snorted. 'Because it may upset Queen Elizabeth. Will Shakespeare gets very worried about that sort of thing. It was he who originally insisted on taking it out after the Revels Office raised concerns about it. And after that Hayward business a couple of years ago, he became even more adamant that we must never perform the scene. He even went so far as to have every copy of it burned – though I've no doubt he kept one for himself. If I went to him with this request, he would refuse. He would also refuse John, Richard, Henry, Robert and anyone else in the company you care to mention. But I don't think he would refuse *you,* Eve.' Gus sniggered, showing his yellow teeth. 'The name rather suits you.'

Alice tried to suppress a wave of nausea. 'Why wouldn't he refuse me?' she managed to ask.

'I saw the way you two talked after *Hamlet.*

He's taken a shine to you, girl, and no mistake.'

It was true – they *had* bonded. The process had begun during the performance when she'd found him in Hell, struggling with that jammed trapdoor, and he'd revealed his insecurity about the play. She realised then that he was a human being, just like her, and she no longer felt so daunted in his presence. Then, when the play was over, he had approached her in the Tiring-House, still in his ghost make-up, and said some very nice things about her performance.

'I'm sure you can persuade him,' beamed Gus, his plump cheeks glowing.

So Gus wanted her to risk her newfound friendship with Mr Shakespeare, all for the sake of his sordid little plot. It was a hideous prospect. She wouldn't do it!

'And if I don't?' she asked.

Gus's face dimmed as if an inner light had been doused. 'Then I have no further use for you. I will inform the others that Adam is, in fact, *Eve*, and Eve will have to leave!'

Chapter 18

Facing the Wall

Will Shakespeare lived just a few minutes walk from the Globe Theatre. He rented a room on the top floor of a lodging house that faced the wall of a prison known as the Clink.

'Whenever I feel trapped by Gus Phillips and his unending demands,' Will explained to Alice, 'I glance out of my window and am reminded of my great good fortune.'

They peered out of his tiny casement at the high, rugged wall that filled most of the other side of the street.

'Do you ever hear the prisoners?' asked Alice.

'Sometimes at night. There's one I call Poor Tom, who raves about the "Foul Fiend" that follows him everywhere. And another who complains constantly about his daughters. I call him Lear.'

Alice giggled at this. 'You must write a play about them, Mr Shakespeare.'

'Maybe I will.'

His room was in the roof of the house, and the ceiling sloped down on both sides of the window. His bed was in one of the eaves. A small writing table stood beneath the window. On its surface a candle flickered, illuminating the loose sheets of a manuscript, a goose-feather quill, an ink pot and a knife for trimming and sharpening the quill.

Alice couldn't resist a glance at the manuscript. The script was neat and firm, filling the whole page with almost no margins. To her surprise, there were no crossings-out.

'Is this a new play?' she asked.

'Aye.'

'What's it about?'

'Two lovers, Troilus and Cressida. It's a tragedy set during the Trojan War.'

'Another tragedy, Mr Shakespeare?'

She pulled a face, and this made him laugh. 'It must be my mood…'

'You should find a more cheerful view,' she suggested. 'It might help your mood.'

'And what view would you recommend for a comedy? A forest? An enchanted island? With views like that, I may not write a thing. It is far better, Adam, to be faced by a wall. For a mind like mine, hungry for distraction, it offers very little sustenance. Faced with this wall, my imagination has no choice but to take wing and alight in places far from here.'

'Like forests or enchanted islands?'

He looked at her. 'Why did you come here, Adam?'

Nervous about revealing the true purpose of her visit, she stalled. 'I'm your friend, aren't I?'

'I hope so,' said Will.

'Then why should I not visit you?'

'For that very reason!' He smiled at her confusion. 'Forgive me,' he said. 'You are a *new* friend, so cannot be expected to know the first rule of being friends with William Shakespeare. My home, Adam, is where I write. Out there is where I see my friends. The only people who bother me at home are the ones who *want* things – usually my money or my words. Do you want something from me, Adam?'

The bright steel of his gaze so rattled her that suddenly all she wanted was to run away. She had been fooled by him. His admission of self-doubt beneath the stage the other day, and those kind words to her after her performance – they had lulled her into believing Will Shakespeare was an ordinary man. But he wasn't. She was reminded of something he had said to her in Wardrobe after she had admitted her fear of playing Ophelia: *Pray hold on to that fear then, if it begets such a face*. This was a man who would sacrifice everything for his art, even friendship. Even family... Edmund had told her how Shakespeare had abandoned his wife and children in Stratford-upon-Avon to pursue a career in London.

'Please forgive me,' she mumbled as she made for the door. 'I will not disturb you any more.'

But the door would not open. Will was holding it closed.

'Did Gus send you here?' he asked.

She gasped. 'How did you know?'

'It's the kind of trick Gus likes to play when he wants something. He must have thought himself so clever sending you here to do his bidding. But he forgets a simple fact: no one at the Globe knows where I live – no one, that is, but *him*.'

Alice hung her head. 'Aye, he sent me. He wants to stage a production of *King Richard II* on Saturday, and he wants to include the dethroning scene. He asks if you would provide him with the script.'

Will did not respond at first. He moved to his desk, fiddled with his quill, gazed out of the window. Finally he asked: 'Did he say why?'

'No.'

He turned to face her. 'Tell him I cannot allow it.'

Alice had been afraid of such a response. A bleak vision of her future arose in her mind – back on the streets, begging for food, this time without Richard.

'Are-Are you sure?' she said, a pleading note entering her voice. 'Gus was very insistent.'

'I'm sure he was,' said Will. 'But Gus must understand: in the current climate, to show the dethroning of a reigning monarch on the stage would be very unwise. It would be like… like igniting a keg of gunpowder. It could spark an uprising. It could close us down. I won't be party to it.'

Alice nodded sadly and opened the door. 'Then I must say goodbye, Mr Shakespeare. It was… a privilege, knowing you.'

'Wait!' said Will. 'What are you talking about?'

'Gus told me that if I couldn't persuade you to hand over the scene, then he would throw me out of the Chamberlain's Men.'

'On what grounds?' cried Will.

'Because…' Alice hesitated – she couldn't tell him the real reason. 'Because he discovered me in his office this morning, going through his confidential papers. I was trying to find out if he knew something about my brother….'

Will looked very despondent at this news. 'That's too bad. I shall miss you, Adam.'

Alice turned quickly and left his room. As she descended the narrow staircase, a great emptiness filled her, and she suppressed a sob. She had nursed a faint hope that Will would relent once he knew what was at stake for her. Why had she thought there was any chance of that? This was *Shakespeare* – the man who sacrificed everything for his art. Of course he would never risk his career for someone like her.

She plodded slowly along the street beneath the prison wall, and it occurred to her that it didn't actually matter which side of the wall she was on. She was a prisoner of fate either way. Her life was over.

No Richard, no Globe, no future…

'Adam! Adam, wait!'

She turned.

Will Shakespeare had run out into the street after her. He was carrying a sheaf of paper.

'Here's the scene!' he panted when he'd caught up with her.

Her heart surged. 'Mr Shakespeare! God grant you mercy! But why did you change your mind?'

'I may live to regret this,' he sighed. 'Strike that! I may not even live, should the queen's men discover the author of this treason.'

Alice bit her lip. 'Then I will not take it,' she said, handing it back to him.

'On the other hand,' said Will, planting it firmly back in her hands, 'one must consider that *A Woman Killed With Kindness* is playing at the Curtain this weekend.'

'I'm sorry, what?'

'And *Satiromastix*, so I hear, is being staged by the Children of Paul's.'

Alice began to suspect that the playwright had lost his wits.

'While down at the Rose, they're putting on *The Blind Beggar of Bethnal Green*,' he continued blithely. 'And *Cynthia's Revels* by Ben Jonson is being revived at Blackfriars. As for the Admirals Men, they're bound to be performing in something at the Fortune…'

'What–What are you talking about, Mr Shakespeare?'

'What I'm talking about, my dear Adam, is this: Will Shakespeare likes to imagine that when his words are spoken at the Globe on a Saturday afternoon, the whole world stops and listens. But Will Shakespeare should remember that his is just one in a competing cacophany of voices, all of them hoping and expecting to be heard. He should remember also the many, many other folk who spurn the playhouses for less wordy diversions like cock fights and the baiting of wild animals. When all of that is considered, he should ask himself: how can one scene in one play affect anything in this world? Did he really imagine it would be a spark to light a conflagration across the city? It is one scene, just a quarter hour in length. It will be forgotten in an even shorter time than that....'

'Are you sure?' asked Alice. The worry lines on his brow seemed to tell a different story – almost as if he was trying to persuade himself of his own argument.

'I admit to some disquiet,' he told her. 'My natural caution goads me to forbid it. But the price of that – the loss of you, my dear friend – would be far too high to bear. Tell Gus he has my blessing to include the scene.'

'Oh, thank you, thank you, Mr Shakespeare!' cried Alice. Her eyes brimming with tears, she hugged him, almost knocking the playwright off his feet. Then she turned and ran down the street towards the river path that would take her back to the Globe.

Chapter 19

The Essex Man

Tom grimaced as he bent to sweep up the cold ashes from the hearth. The cuts and bruises on his back hurt worse than ever when they chafed against his shirt. He had taken the beating of his life yesterday. Twenty strokes from Sir Gelly Meyrick's whip – the price for deserting his duties on Tuesday afternoon.

His invented excuse – that he'd spotted an intruder and taken off in pursuit – had not been enough to save him, for it could not account for the nearly three hours he had been missing. So Tom had taken his punishment. He had tried hard not to cry, but by the tenth or eleventh stroke the pain was so great he could not stop himself. By the twentieth, he was very nearly unconscious, and had to be helped from the room by another servant. That night he had lain curled up on his truckle bed in his tiny attic room as waves of agony rippled through his broken, blistering flesh.

Now, after being given just a day to recover, Tom was back at his duties. When the hearth was swept, he struggled with the heavy bucket of ashes to the kitchen where he sifted out the cinders for reuse in the oven, then dumped the remains in the midden behind the kitchen yard. After that, he set to work polishing the silverware.

It could have been so much worse, he reflected. If his fellow servants Amy and Owen had mentioned the mysterious new groom they'd spotted in Tom's company that afternoon, he might have been forced to confess everything. That would have spelt the end of his service at Essex House or anywhere else. In the circumstances, a beating had been the best he could expect.

Yet despite the risks he'd taken, and the punishment he had received, he knew he would do it all again – that was the strangest part. Helping Adam, deciphering the mysteries of *The Ambassadors*, locating the priest hole, uncovering a secret plot, spending time with Sir Francis Bacon – it all added up to one of the most thrilling days of his life. And the adventure was far from over. The consequences of the secret meeting between Sir Gelly, Lord Monteagle and Augustus Phillips had still to play themselves out. If his theory was correct, the performance of *King Richard II* would prepare the ground for a rebellion – not just against the hated Beagle, but against the queen herself, and her entire government. This was deeply troubling to Tom. For his master, the Earl of Essex, *loved* the queen, and longed for nothing more than to win back her favour. Surely he could not be a party to this plot?

Should he warn the earl? But what if he did so and it turned out that the earl knew all about it. The question would then arise: how did Tom find out? His spying activities would come to light, and his career, perhaps even his life, would be over. Better, he thought, to say nothing for now and keep his eyes and ears open. He was reminded of a line from *Hamlet*: 'Give every man thy ear, but few thy voice.'

'How do you fare today, young man?'

Tom turned at the lilting tone of Sir Gelly's Welsh accent.

'I am well, sir,' he said.

Sir Gelly came closer and picked up a silver dish that Tom had been polishing. 'This is good – it really sparkles!' he said.

He didn't usually praise Tom's work. Was this, perhaps, his way of attempting to mend relations between them after the beating? Yet Tom felt no resentment towards the steward. The punishment had been fair.

They were in a chamber off the Great Hall containing some of the earl's most prized possessions, whether for banquets or battles. Sir Gelly wandered along one wall hung with swords and shields. He plucked a rapier from its hook and examined it for a moment. Suddenly, he threw it across the room towards Tom. Without thinking, Tom dropped his polishing cloth and caught the weapon. He quickly transferred his hand from the blade to the hilt.

'You can fight, can't you Tom?' said Sir Gelly.

'Not really, sir,' Tom replied.

'Come now, Tom, don't be so modest. Sir John told me what a promising student you are.'

Sir John Davies was a former soldier of fortune, knighted by the earl for his services to him, and now a member of his household. It was true, he had given Tom a few lessons with the sword.

Now, Sir Gelly drew his own rapier. 'Let's see if he is right, shall we?'

'Sir, I...'

'What is it, Tom? Are you scared?'

Sir Gelly's sword was raised, ready for engagement. But Tom, with his sore back, was in no mood to fight.

'I'm not feeling my best today, sir.'

'You just said you were well.'

The steward made a thrust towards Tom's midriff. It was a half-hearted attack, which Tom easily parried. Yet even this movement sent a flash of pain through the welts on his shoulders.

Sir Gelly began circling Tom, who was forced to turn slowly on the spot in order to keep facing him. The steward was a big man with a smiling, fleshy face that gleamed with sweat. He was bouncing on his toes and looked primed to launch another attack. Tom wondered if he had been at the wine.

Tom had his right foot forward, his left a shoulder's width behind, as Sir John had taught him. He kept his knees slightly bent and the weight centred between his legs. *The stance is your base and all movement starts from there.* He forced himself to remain upright, even though his instincts were to lean backwards, away from the rapier tip that wobbled in the air before his nose.

The next attack was a cut to Tom's right side – his flank. He raised his sword just in time and caught the blow in the forte of his blade (the part closest to the hilt). It sent a sharp and painful jolt up his arm and across his back. This was followed, much more shockingly, by a thrust towards his face. Tom jerked his head backwards, flinging up his off-hand (his left) to parry. His palm stung from its forceful impact with the tip.

Now he was scared. *Did Sir Gelly mean to kill him?*

The steward came at him next with a series of complicated cuts and thrusts, his blade flashing as it swished one way, then the other. Tom parried these as best he could, both with his sword and off-hand, but he was being forced into a jerky, stumbling retreat.

'Fight me, boyo!' cried Sir Gelly. 'Don't just defend. Fight!'

'Please, sir, I cannot do this!'

With each strike, Sir Gelly seemed to get closer to Tom's flesh. And Tom's defences were weakening.

The constant parrying was sending repeated shockwaves through his bones, and he could feel the scabs breaking in his back and fresh blood mingling with the sweat.

Finally, Tom, now in excruciating pain, collided with the wall. Unable to retreat any further, he stood there, nose to nose with Sir Gelly, the forte of the steward's blade thrust hard against his hilt. Panting now, Sir Gelly whispered: 'You don't think much of me, do you, Tom?'

'That's not true, sir,' groaned Tom, flinching from the powerful garlic-and-ale smell of Sir Gelly's breath.

'You must think me pretty stupid in fact!'

'Of course not!'

'Then why did you lie to me about running after the intruder?'

Tom closed his eyes. *So that was what this was all about!*

Sir Gelly pushed harder with his sword, forcing Tom's blade back against his own cheek. 'Owen told me he spied you in the picture gallery in the company of someone else dressed as a groom – someone he had never seen before. Who was it, Tom? And what were you doing in the picture gallery?'

Tom's mouth opened, but no words came out. What could he say?

Sir Gelly stepped back. His face relaxed, and for a moment, Tom thought he was about to be let go with a warning. But then the steward brought the tip of his rapier down hard against Tom's wrist. With a yelp of pain, Tom dropped his sword, which fell with a clatter to the floor. Sir Gelly's blade was pointing at his chest, its tip grazing the fabric of his doublet. 'The width of three fingers…' growled the steward. 'That's as far as I need to thrust this blade into your body to kill you. And I will – unless you answer my questions!'

Tom's mind was in a frenzy as he tried to think of what to say. If he told Sir Gelly about Adam, then Adam might be killed to prevent him from exposing their plot. At all costs, he had to keep Adam out of this. What would satisfy Sir Gelly? What story was he expecting to hear…?

And then it came to him, and it was so perfect, it was difficult not to smile.

'It was the Beagle's doing, sir.'

'What?' barked Sir Gelly, his eyes flaring dangerously. Tom felt the tip of his sword pressing ever more firmly against his chest. His next words would have to be chosen very carefully.

'Lord Cecil didn't only leave those eight yeomen behind on Tuesday, sir. He–He also left behind a spy – a spy dressed as a groom. The groom took me captive and–and forced me, on pain of death, to show him where the priest hole was. He knew – I don't know how, sir, but he knew – that there was a priest hole at Essex House and that Lord Monteagle was hiding in it. I panicked, sir, under his questioning and I let slip that I'd heard you and his lordship mention that a priest hole was built somewhere in the picture gallery.

But I swear I never told him Lord Monteagle was in there!'

The pressure from the sword tip intensified and Tom felt its piercing sharpness against his breast bone. Just a touch more force and he would be impaled.

'Go on!' barked Sir Gelly.

'So he–he forced me to go there with him. Of course I couldn't find it – I knew I would never find something so well hidden. Finally, he left, full of anger and warnings. He told me if I ever breathed a word of this to anyone, he would come back and kill me. That was why I lied to you, sir. I was scared! I beseech you, Sir Gelly, please forgive me!' Tom felt the tears on his cheeks. They were from the pain in his chest, but they were also timely, he realised, for they lent credence to his words.

At last he felt the pressure from the blade start to lessen, and his lungs began to work again. But Sir Gelly's stern expression showed no sign of easing. 'That wily little schemer!' he snarled. 'The Beagle thought he could catch us with this underhand trick. I should have seen it coming!'

With relief, Tom realised that the steward's anger was no longer directed at him – indeed he seemed almost to have forgotten Tom's existence. The story, invented under extreme pressure, had produced the desired result. It had worked because Sir Gelly really did fear the Beagle and believed him entirely capable of this kind of intrigue.

Finally, Sir Gelly's gaze refocused on Tom, and his expression softened. 'Next time, tell the truth, boyo,' he said. 'You're an Essex man, same as me. You must be prepared to die for him, if necessary. Would you die for your master, Tom?'

'Aye, sir,' said Tom with as much conviction as he could muster. He felt wretched, with pains in his chest, wrist and across his back. But would he die for the earl – truly? What if he was part of the plot? Would he follow him even in a rebellion against the Queen of England? Tom was sickened by the thought of having to make such a choice.

Suddenly, he was seized by the desire to run away – to escape from Essex House, with its dreadful atmosphere of resentment, fear and suspicion. But where could he go? The Globe? It would be wonderful to be able to spend more time with Adam – yet he could not imagine himself fitting in there among the painted players, spouting made-up words each day for the diversion of the London mob. What about York House? Aye! That was where he would go. Sir Francis liked him. He would take him in. He could assist the philosopher in his experiments – help him build a seeing-tube to learn the secrets of the moon. He could read the books in his library and they could sit like gentlemen and discuss the mysteries of the universe. He could become a scholar!

Sir Gelly scooped up Tom's rapier and threw it back to him. Fumblingly, Tom caught it. 'Keep practising,' the steward advised him. 'The next time Lord Cecil comes, he will come in force. We must be ready for him – which means every man of fighting age should know how to wield a weapon. You will fight and die for your master, do you understand me, Tom?'

Chapter 20
Whitehall Palace

'By royal command, we are invited to Whitehall Palace for a performance of *Hamlet*!' grinned Gus Phillips, brandishing a heavily embossed vellum scroll. His words were greeted with enthusiastic cheers and some laughter. Everyone was there in the Tiring-House – sharers, prentices and hired men – seated on stools or lounging against the walls.

'The play's the thing, wherein we'll catch the praises of a queen!' chuckled Richard Burbage, deliberately misquoting a line spoken by his character.

'You see, Will, your Danish play has a future after all – at least the palace seems to think so!' said John Heminges, another sharer.

'Perhaps they heard the laughter at Polonius's

death and thought it a comedy,' said Shakespeare with a rueful smile.

When the guffaws that followed this had died down, Gus announced: 'I will go the palace this afternoon to discuss arrangements for the performance. Burbage, will you join me? We all saw how taken the queen was by your Prince Hal when we performed *Henry IV Part 1* for her four years ago, so feel free to lay on the charm!'

Alice smiled along with everyone else at this remark, though she did so purely out of courtesy. She doubted that anything would ever amuse her again while her brother remained missing. If only she could get away from here and continue her search for him. Almost a week had passed since his disappearance, and she would probably have accepted the fact of his death by now, had it not been for the discovery of the locket. Did he drop it there for her to find? The secret code might provide the answer. Alice wondered if Sir Francis Bacon had made any progress with it.

'And if we're to take our Hamlet, we should also bring along his Ophelia,' said Gus, catching Alice's eye.

She gave a start. *The palace? She couldn't possibly…*

'It will show our royal patron that the Chamberlain's Men have a future, with fresh young talent waiting in the wings,' he explained to the others, while keeping his beady eyes fixed on her.

'Don't forget the "fresh *old* talent",' muttered Robert Armin. 'We're not quite dead yet!'

This provoked more laughter. Alice smiled along

politely as her heart raced. She would see the inside of Whitehall Palace – the very seat of royal power – and maybe even meet the queen! But why had *she,* a mere prentice, been selected for this honour instead of one of the other sharers? Did Gus really want her there as a representative of the next generation – or was it, as she suspected, that he no longer trusted her and wanted to keep her close to him at all times?

Alice had nothing to wear but her usual drab boy-clothes, so Gus handed her over to Tim in Wardrobe, and she emerged half an hour later in a beautifully embroidered cream doublet with a high, stiff collar, dark red sleeves with matching trunk hose and thigh-length stockings. A dark, fashionably short cloak hung from her shoulders.

A specially ordered barge was waiting at the Paris Garden steps to convey them to the palace. It was a beautiful vessel, with six liveried oarsmen, and prow, stern and rail gilded and carved with the royal coat of arms bordered by fanciful sea creatures, swags and scrolls. The barge began to edge its way towards the middle of the river, as wherry-boats scrambled to keep out of its way. The passengers reclined on soft velvet cushions. Gus lit up his pipe while Richard Burbage pretended he was Julius Caesar on a triumph, waving at the Roman crowds. Alice sat quietly, wishing Richard was with her and wondering what one ought to say when meeting the queen.

The Thames wound slowly south, and soon, on its northern bank, the spectacular frontage of Whitehall Palace came into view. Flags streamed from its tall turrets, and a set of balustraded stone steps led down to the river. They were greeted at these steps by servants dressed in velvet, fur, cloth of gold, silk and lace – materials that no servants but the queen's were allowed to wear, for the sumptuary laws forbade such extravagance. Guards were also present in helmets and chest armour and armed with long pikes. More guards were in evidence in the palace forecourt, marching and standing sentry. The palace looked very secure, and Alice wondered how Monteagle and his fellow conspirators thought they had any chance of seizing the throne by force.

The guests were led through a portcullised gateway into a vast courtyard. After mounting some more steps they passed through a set of iron-studded oak doors and were ushered down a long corridor, then through a series of rooms, each more spectacular than the last. Alice wished she could have lingered to appreciate the exotic tapestries, gold ceilings and spectacular paintings. She glimpsed a huge stained-glass window showing the stages of Christ's passion; a mother-of-pearl organ; the bauble and bell of King Henry VIII's court jester; and a portrait of the queen's late brother, Edward VI, as a little boy.

They ascended some stairs into a gallery that overlooked the tilt yard where jousts took place. From here they passed through the queen's private quarters – her bedchamber and dressing-room. Alice gasped to see her gilded bath tub and how the water gushed out of oyster shells. In a room called the Wonder-Cabinet, they found objects from every corner of the world, with inscriptions to identify them. They included a statuette of an Ethiopian riding a rhinoceros, an Indian axe and canoe, a chain of monkey teeth and the tail of a unicorn.

The journey through the enormous, labyrinthine palace finally ended in a small antechamber, where they were told to wait. After a short time, an official entered. He told them he was about to lead them into the queen's presence. They should bow as they enter, and not stare at her. On no account should they approach her but should always remain at least six paces from her person, unless she chose to approach them. They should not speak unless spoken to, and address her as 'Your Majesty' and subsequently as 'Ma'am'.

Her heart thumping madly, Alice followed the others into a small room with panelled walls and lit with candles that reflected in the gilded frames of paintings. There was a heavy scent of roses. At the far end, seated on a dais and flanked by several courtiers and ladies in waiting, was the Queen of England.

Chapter 21

A Surprising Revelation

Seeing the queen made Alice feel dizzy and breathless, as if she had climbed to some spectacularly high place, close to the planets and stars. Two years ago she had been begging on the streets of London. It didn't seem possible that she was now standing here in this room, breathing the same air as the queen.

Alice had seen plenty of portraits of her. She was familiar with her milk-white countenance and vivid red hair. Yet the portraits always showed a woman with a face that was young or somehow ageless, as if carved from marble. The queen was now sixty-seven, and showing her years. Her face was long and gaunt with wrinkles visible behind the white mask. The hair was clearly a wig. Even so, she presented a spectacular vision. Her dress of white and crimson with silver gauze had slashed sleeves lined with red taffeta. The collar of her robe was very high and its lining was adorned with rubies and pearls. More rubies and pearls were hung about her neck and she wore a chain of tiny jewels upon her forehead.

Gus, Richard and Alice bowed deeply, and then the queen rose from her throne and approached them. She had a slim, elegant figure, Alice noted, and a nose that was slightly hooked. Her sprightly movements reminded Alice of a small, exotic bird. Gus bowed once more as she came close, and kissed the hem of her robe. 'Your majesty…' he gushed.

'Mr Phillips! How delightful to see you again.' She laid a hand upon his arm. The hand was small, with veins visible beneath almost translucent skin. On spotting Richard Burbage, she smiled, causing wrinkles to form around her mouth, and her eyes shimmered with pleasure. 'Mr Burbage, your Hamlet is the talk of the town. I can't wait to see it for myself.'

'Your majesty, you flatter me. We will do our best to make our performance here at the palace our most memorable yet.'

'Ma'am, may I introduce one of our newest and youngest players, Adam Fletcher,' said Gus, indicating Alice.

The queen swivelled, and her deep brown eyes locked with Alice's. Alice blushed and made an awkward bow.

'And what part will you play, young man?' asked

the queen.

'Ophelia, your majesty.'

At this point, one of the courtiers standing on the dais approached the queen. He was a very short man – even shorter than Alice – with a long face that appeared even longer due to his pointed beard and swept-back hair. He had thin lips and dark eyes that flicked restlessly between Gus, Richard and Alice, even as he addressed the queen. 'Your majesty, would you grant me a few minutes with Mr Phillips to talk through some matters relating to security on the day?'

'Take him, Lord Cecil,' answered the queen.

So this was Lord Cecil, the Chief Minister… Alice had glimpsed him galloping away across the courtyard of Essex House three days ago. He had been trying to find Lord Monteagle that day. How interested would he be to know that Gus Phillips – the man he now wished to speak to – had met with Monteagle just a short while later?

'Take young Adam, too,' added the queen, 'but leave me with Mr Burbage, if you please. I wish to hear him recite that speech from *Richard III*, when he woos the Lady Anne.' She smiled coquettishly at Burbage, revealing a few missing teeth.

Gus and Alice bowed to the queen, and then Lord Cecil ushered them through a door. He led them at a rapid pace along a dim, narrow corridor to another room. It was colder in here, despite the fire that snapped and spat in the hearth. There was a dark patina to the room's oak furniture and panelling that made Alice feel gloomy and slightly unsettled. Perhaps it was the wind gusting through the casement, but the candlelight seemed to judder rather than flicker, causing long, jerky shadows to shift along the walls and floor.

Lord Cecil seated himself at a dark, almost black table. On the wall behind him hung a rather severe coat of arms with the motto *Sero, sed serio*.

'Thank you for agreeing to meet me, your grace,' said Gus.

'You are most welcome,' replied Cecil. 'What do you wish to tell me?'

Alice stared at the two of them in surprise. From the way they were talking, it seemed that Gus, not Lord Cecil, had wanted this meeting. Was there some other purpose, then, to this visit to the palace?

'I have some grave news for you,' said Gus. 'I have learned of a plot to destabilise her majesty's government.'

Hearing this, Alice's mouth went very dry. The fire popped in the grate, and the air turned a touch chillier. Lord Cecil remained impassive, his hawklike eyes fixed unblinkingly upon Gus. Very slowly, they swivelled towards Alice.

'You are telling me this in front of the boy?'

Gus half-smiled, and Alice caught a dangerous gleam in the jaundiced whites of his eyes. 'The *boy* can be trusted,' he chuckled, and the emphasis he placed on 'boy' told Alice exactly why he felt so sure of this.

'In that case,' said Cecil, 'tell me what you know, Mr Phillips.'

'Three days ago,' said Gus, 'I was called to a meeting at Essex House. Lord Monteagle and Sir Gelly Meyrick, the steward, were present.'

Alice noticed Cecil stiffen at the mention of Monteagle. She herself was in a state of shock that Gus was making this confession. *Was he not one of the conspirators?*

'Is Monteagle still at Essex House?' Cecil asked.

'No,' replied Gus. 'He departed straight after the meeting – said he planned to "lie low" for a while.'

For the first time, Alice saw a flicker of frustration disturb Lord Cecil's face. Monteagle had slipped his grasp once again.

Gus continued: 'They asked me if my company would put on a performance of Shakespeare's play, *King Richard II*, on Saturday – which is tomorrow. I complained that it is an old play and unlikely to attract a big audience; we would have to dust off costumes and relearn our parts. So they offered me forty shillings on top of our normal takings as an inducement. But they insisted that we include the banned scene – the one in which…'

'I know the scene,' interjected Lord Cecil. 'Did they mention if the earl was aware of their plans?'

'They said it was his idea, sire.'

'You know why he's doing this, don't you, Mr Phillips?'

'Clearly, he wishes to sew the seeds of rebellion

in the minds of the people,' replied Gus. 'For many, Essex remains a hero, and it will be easy for them to imagine him in the role of Bolingbroke...'

'And the queen in the role of Richard II.'

Gus did not respond – he merely dipped his head, perhaps fearful of giving verbal assent to such a disturbing idea.

'They are softening up the populace for a seizure of power,' said Lord Cecil. 'They want to show them, graphically, upon the stage, that such a thing is possible – even desirable. That 1601 can be 1399. This is the prelude to the rebellion that I knew was coming. You must not perform this play, Mr Phillips.'

'Sire, may I suggest a contrary view – that we *should* perform the play.'

'And why is that?' frowned Cecil.

'Because it will give you the evidence you need against your enemy, Essex... I know what he has been up to, sire. He's been fortifying his house, recruiting an army, giving hospitality to troublemakers like Monteagle and Southampton. Yet despite all of this, the queen continues to indulge him – he is, after all, her former favourite. He still loves her, or so she believes.'

'You are very well informed, Mr Phillips,' muttered Cecil dryly.

'But now he has gone too far,' continued Gus. 'He has commissioned a performance in a public playhouse that is an incitement to rebellion. This is an act of open defiance against her authority. After this, even her majesty will be forced to conclude that the Earl of Essex has become a danger to the realm.'

Cecil said nothing, waiting for Gus to go on.

'Come to the Globe tomorrow afternoon, sire. Sit in the audience and see for yourself the effect of the play on the crowd. Then you can go back to the queen and explain to her with all the authority of an eye-witness, why this man must be stopped – and stopped quickly – before the terrible deeds represented on the stage come to pass on the streets of London and, dare I say it, in this very palace.'

'Sir Gelly Meyrick and others from Essex House will be at the Globe tomorrow, I take it?'

'I am certain of it,' said Gus.

'Then I shall go to your play, together with a detachment of yeomen, and I shall arrest the plotters immediately upon its conclusion,' declared Cecil.

'If you arrive with a detachment of yeomen, sire, then the performance, most likely, will be cancelled, and your quarry will simply melt away into the Southwark mob. May I propose that you would do better to adopt a lower profile, so as not to raise the alarm.'

Cecil nodded thoughtfully. 'You make a powerful argument, sirrah. I will think on what you say.'

'One more thing, sire: I beg you not to forget who brought this information to you. I am, and will always remain, your loyal servant. I ask for no personal reward, only the continuing honour and privilege of her majesty's patronage.'

Alice smiled to herself when she heard this. So that was why Gus had betrayed the plot – to keep the support of the queen and her chief minister.

'And that you shall have, Mr Phillips, that you shall have,' said Cecil vaguely – for the matter of patronage was the least of his concerns. Alice could tell that he was already considering what his strategy should be for the following day. Her instincts told her he was planning something quite dramatic.

Act Four

7th ~ 8th February 1601

Chapter 22

Outside the Playhouse

The crowd that jammed the concourse outside the Globe was huge – bigger even than the one Tom had witnessed on his previous visit five days earlier. It was also rowdy, with its chanting and frequent surges of movement. Tom wondered whether the people sensed that something was afoot?

'Stay close, boyo!' Sir Gelly urged him as they attempted to push their way towards the entrance. 'Once we're inside, we can escape the fray and take our seats in the gallery.'

A red flag fluttered from the roof of the Globe, indicating that today's entertainment would be a history play. Playbills pinned to the exterior of the building advertised:

THE
Tragedie of King
Richard the Second
by William Shakespeare

A new PERFORMANCE
by the Lord Chamberlain's Men

'Today's the day when our plans will start to bear fruit, Tom,' Sir Gelly had told him that morning. 'We're going to see a play at the Globe – a show for the people, so they can see for themselves how tyranny can be overthrown and a true leader can emerge. It will plant a seed in the people's minds, from which will sprout a revolution.'

So they had overheard the conversation correctly in the priest hole! Still, it had been a shock to hear Sir Gelly move so quickly from talk of defending Essex House to a declaration of open rebellion. Feigning innocence, Tom had replied: 'Really, sir! How so?'

'You'll see, boyo. Watch and learn. The play is Shakespeare's *King Richard II*. For King Richard, read Queen Elizabeth. For Bolingbroke, read the Earl of Essex.'

Tom had felt compelled to object: 'But sir, the queen is no tyrant. I thought our enemy was Lord Cecil.'

With a sad shake of his head, Sir Gelly had replied: 'The two are now so entwined as to be inseparable. She will no longer abide to listen to any voice but his.'

Tossed about on the tides of people, Tom felt both excited and scared. He was pleased to be back here, and hoped he might see Adam again. But the crowd was intimidating. What kind of monster was Sir Gelly unleashing, and did he really think he could control it?

'See there!' said Sir Gelly, pointing out a tall, wild-looking man with a forked beard. 'Our supporters are gathering.' The man, Tom noticed, was wearing a brooch that bore Essex's coat of arms – a shield surrounded by a blue circle and topped by a crown.

As Tom looked more closely at those around him, he started to see several familiar figures: the soldiers of fortune who had been mustering in the courtyard of Essex House.

Essex's men had come to the Globe, Tom guessed, to cheer the moment of the king's dethroning and incite the audience to do likewise. This was a call to arms to the people of London. But would it be heeded?

It was true that the queen was not popular. The zenith of her power and authority was long in the past. Tom was too young to remember the famous victory over the Spanish Armada twelve summers ago, but he had heard about it from Sir Gelly, Sir John and the earl himself. Back then, the entire kingdom had been united in its adulation of Good Queen Bess. Yet in the years since, that love had soured. The country had been cursed by a terrible run of harvests, and the government had embarked on a series of expensive foreign wars. Prices had risen, and many had been plunged into poverty. Tom did not have to stray far from Essex House or the Strand to find streets where the homeless and malnourished begged for scraps. But the queen saw nothing of this. She had retreated behind the well-guarded doors of her luxurious palaces, and did not see how her people suffered.

Essex saw it, though – according to Sir Gelly. Essex had lived and fought alongside ordinary men and he understood their plight. That was the reason why he was so popular. A modern Bolingbroke, Sir Gelly called him. *But do the people see him that way?* Tom wondered. *And will a single scene in a play really be enough to trigger an uprising?*

Finally, they reached the entrance. Above it was a crest with the words *Totus mundus agit histrionem*. '"The whole world is a playhouse",' Tom translated.

'You mean "All the world's a stage",' said someone close by. 'It's from *As You Like It*, a play by Shakespeare.' The voice was small and light, and it sounded familiar. Tom looked around to see who had spoken, but saw no one among the anonymous faces who was looking in his direction. By the time he faced front again, several others had squeezed in ahead of him in the queue. He glimpsed Sir Gelly beyond them, paying the gatherer the entrance fee. Tom struggled to reach him, but a wall of bodies blocked his way.

He felt a tap on his shoulder and turned once more. There stood Adam. Tom felt a flush of happiness at the sight of his friend. He had missed him these past few days. 'Come with me!' said Adam.

Happily, he followed Adam out of the queue. *I'll feel the sting of Sir Gelly's whip for this*, he told himself, and for some reason the thought scarcely troubled him.

They walked at a rapid pace around the curve of the playhouse's external wall. 'It's happening just as we thought it would, isn't it?' Tom said excitedly. 'There's bound to be a riot when King Richard gets dethroned.'

Adam stopped and looked gravely at Tom. 'And you're happy about that, are you?'

'Well...' Tom trailed away. The truth was, he was quite nervous.

'I pulled you out of the playhouse because I wanted to get you away in case of trouble.'

'Oh, you didn't have to worry about me,' Tom grinned. 'It's the government that ought to be scared.'

Adam didn't return the smile. 'Gus went to Lord Cecil yesterday. He told him everything.'

'What?' Tom rocked back in surprise. 'Then why is the play still going ahead?'

'Gus persuaded Cecil to let us perform it. He said Cecil should use it as a way of bringing down your master. It'll be the first bit of actual evidence he's gathered that Essex is planning a rebellion. But I don't think Cecil's in an evidence-gathering mood. He's going to send in his soldiers, I'm sure of it, as soon as we perform the banned scene. He'll arrest Sir Gelly and anyone with him. That's why I had to get you out of there.'

'I have to warn Sir Gelly,' muttered Tom.

Adam looked disappointed. 'Whose side are you on, Tom? Sir Gelly wants to depose our queen. Do you really think he still deserves your loyalty?'

Tom didn't know *what* to think any more. He wished Sir Francis could be here to advise them. 'I've sworn an oath of loyalty to my master,' he said.

'And does your master know what Sir Gelly is up to?'

'I'm not sure.'

'Well, until you are, wouldn't it be better to play safe?'

Tom thought this sounded reasonable. Still, Adam's certainty about what was best for him was beginning to chafe on his nerves. Adam was just a boy, no older than him. What did he know?

'I'm grateful to you for the warning,' he said, 'but my place is with Sir Gelly. And if Cecil's men come for us, I'll be ready for them.' He indicated the sword that hung from his belt. 'I'm a trained swordsman…' It wasn't strictly true, but he wanted Adam to understand that he could look after himself.

Adam gave a mirthless smile. 'You may be William Marshall for all I know. It won't make a difference.

You won't be able to defeat a dozen yeomen when they come at you at once. Come with me, Tom. Hide out backstage until the play is over. Then we can work out what to do next.'

'No,' said Tom. His jaw trembled with all he wanted to say. But how did one explain a sense of duty, and the love and compassion he felt for his master? If Adam only knew the terrible humiliations that the earl had been forced to endure at the hands of the Beagle, perhaps he would understand. But there was no time to explain all of that – he had to get back to Sir Gelly.

As he turned to go, a door opened at the back of the building – the same door through which he had entered on his previous visit backstage. A young man, a few years older than him, stepped out. He was dressed in a short tunic and colourful hose that seemed to belong to another century.

'Adam!' he called when he caught sight of him. 'I thought I heard your voice out here. Where have you been? I've been looking for you.'

'Edmund!' said Adam. 'This is Tom.'

The youth nodded at Tom, then turned back to Adam. 'I have something for you,' he said, handing him a scroll.

Tom, not waiting to hear any more, continued on his way.

'It's got a fancy seal on it,' he heard Edmund say.

Then Adam's surprised voice exclaimed: 'It's from Sir Francis Bacon!'

Tom stopped in his tracks.

Sir Francis! The code!

He spun around and raced back to the other two just as Adam split the seal.

Chapter 23

The Secret Message

Alice had to resist opening the letter from Sir Francis there and then behind the Globe. The place was too public. She led Edmund and Tom through the door Edmund had just come through, into a messy backroom of the playhouse. Here, she seated herself on an upturned witch's cauldron while the other two took up position behind her, peering over her shoulder as she unfurled the letter. There were two sheets enclosed – a letter from Sir Francis and the original document, containing the code, that he had borrowed. Alice turned to Sir Francis's letter first, and they all took a moment to admire the elegance of the calligraphy that filled the parchment. Then they began to read.

York House
7 February 1601

To Adam Fletcher and Tom Cavendish

Greetings, my young friends, I hope this finds you well. I have spent every night since your visit striving to decipher the coded message that you left with me. I have attempted several classic decryption methods, and here are the results of my endeavours.

The Spartan Scytale
My first approach was the Spartan scytale. This is a wooden staff around which a strip of paper containing coded letters can be wound. If it is of the right thickness, then the letters on the strip of paper will align to form a message. I tried staffs of many and varied thicknesses, yet in no case was any message revealed.

The Caesar Cipher
Next, I wondered if the code could be a Caesar cipher, by which I mean that one letter stands for another. In a Caesar cipher, the letter A might stand for D, and B might stand for E, for example. This kind of cipher can be solved by looking at how frequently certain letters appear. We know that E is the most common letter in our language, followed by T and then A. If this had been a Caesar cipher, I could have hunted for the most frequently used letter in the code and called that E, and so on down the list. I spent many hours on this, but failed to find any message.

Invisible ink

After that, my investigations turned to the paper itself. Was it possible that some invisible message had been written there using plant milk, the juice of a lemon, or some other similar substance? I gently warmed the paper under the flame of a candle to see what might be revealed. Sadly, this, too, yielded no results.

My friends, it pains me to report that the document has thus far resisted all my methods. In my bones, I sense that the illustration of the carriage and the flash of lightning provides a clue. Carriages create parallel tracks, do they not? The lightning suggests a zigzag.

If I had but more time I would explore these approaches. Alas I have not. Yet I beseech you both to persist with this for I am certain that there is meaning to be found within these disordered letters. Please do keep me informed should you discover anything.

Your affectionate friend,

Francis Bacon

Alice sighed and let the letter slip into her lap. If the finest mind in England couldn't crack the code, then what chance did *they* have?

Edmund was the first to speak. He wanted to know how Alice had managed to persuade someone so high-ranking as Sir Francis Bacon to help her with her message, and also what Tom had to do with all this.

So Alice and Tom described to him everything that had happened over the past few days, and Edmund's mouth grew wider and wider as he listened. When they had finished, he shook his head in wonder. 'Are you saying that Richard's disappearance, the coded message and the play we're performing today are all connected?'

'Deeply connected,' said Alice.

'And our play is the opening shot in a rebellion against the queen?'

'That's what we believe,' said Tom.

'God's teeth! That is… extraordinary!'

A trumpet sounded somewhere high above them.

'Fie on me!' cried Edmund. 'The play has begun and I am in the second scene!' Dashing to the door, he turned and added: 'For my own part, I think Sir Francis gave up much too easily. The code is almost certainly a Caesar cipher. Keep looking!' Then he turned and ran from the room.

'Are *you* not playing a part in the play?' Tom asked Alice.

'Thankfully not,' she replied. 'And no special effects are needed today either. The *effects* are all in the words, as Will Shakespeare is fond of saying.'

'That will certainly be true when the dethronement scene is performed,' said Tom. Alice was relieved to note that he did not seem half so excited about the prospect as earlier. 'When will it come, by the way?'

'In Act IV,' she replied.

'We have some time then – before all hell breaks loose!'

'Will you go and warn Sir Gelly?' she asked him.

Tom frowned. His jaw tightened. 'No,' he said finally. 'First, I want to help you break this code.'

They both stared at it, willing the gibberish to make sense.

goefburrcadiilegethsvrsibiewbetrlaeldtsiekldlvrrfbsesglb7erayibriklbalateeodwtnnonrabeesaluyrtsileieeotinsae

As Edmund had suggested, they tried the Caesar cipher again, experimentally trying different letters in place of others. Nothing worked. Soon the letters were starting to blur. It was becoming hard to concentrate. Alice squeezed her eyes shut, then opened them once more on the now-familiar letters of the code. She forced herself to concentrate.

Carriages create parallel tracks… That was what Sir Francis had said. *Parallel tracks*…

Quickly, she counted up the letters. *One hundred and eight. That could make two parallel lines of… fifty four.*

'We need writing materials,' she said, jumping out of her chair.

'What for?' asked Tom.

'You'll see…' She dashed from the room.

For the second time that week, Alice sneaked into Gus's office. This time she only remained there long enough to find a quill that worked, a bottle of iron-gall ink and a scrap of rag-paper. Back in the props room, she kneeled on the floor, leaned her paper against the overturned cauldron, and began to write out the code, this time across two lines of fifty-four letters each.

goefburrcadiilegethsvrsihiewbetrlaeldtsiekldlvrrfhsesg
lh7erayihriklhalateeodwtnnonraheesaluyrtsileieeotinsae

'Why have you done that?' asked Tom, once she'd finished.

'Parallel tracks,' said Alice.

'Aye,' said Tom. 'And?'

They looked at each other. Then, to Alice's acute discomfort, Tom burst out laughing.

'I'm sorry,' he said, wiping his eyes. 'It's just… I can see why you did it, but I don't see how it helps. We've now got two equal-length lines of gobbledegook instead of one. But we're no further forward.'

Alice went very tight inside. Heat flooded her cheeks and she slammed down her quill. A fine spray of ink droplets splashed across the page. They formed a fan of thin black lines, covering some of the letters.

'See what you made me do!' she said crossly.

'I don't see how that was my fault,' said Tom, frowning at the mess she'd made.

'You made me angry,' sulked Alice.

But Tom wasn't listening. He was now staring at the paper – at the spray of thin black lines, and at the letters.

Reluctantly, Alice followed his gaze. Try as she might, she couldn't work out what had caught his interest.

'The lightning strike,' whispered Tom.

'What of it?' she asked.

'See that line of ink your quill made there. See how it's connected the first letter of the top line – the *g* – to the first letter of the lower line – the *l*.'

She looked, and saw what he meant.

'And that other line of ink has joined the same *l* to the *o* next to the *g*.'

He was right. But so what?

'*g*...*l*...*o*...' said Tom. 'It sounds like the beginning of a word, doesn't it? And look at the pattern...' He traced out the three letters with his finger. 'It's the start of a lightning strike – a zigzag – don't you see?'

Tom continued to chart this same zigzag course across the two lines of letters with his forefinger, calling them out as he went. Alice picked up the pen and began jotting down the letters as he called them. From the *o*, he dropped down to the second letter of the lower line (*b*), then diagonally upwards to the third letter of the top line (*e*).

'Stop!' cried Alice. 'You've just spelled *globe*. That's the first sensible word we've found.'

Tom laughed. 'You're a genius, Adam, and I was a fool to doubt you! If you hadn't written out the letters this way...'

'*And* spilled the ink,' she reminded him.

'You said *I* was to blame for that!'

'Let's just call it a joint discovery,' she smiled. 'Now, please continue reading out those letters.'

Tom did so, and before long they had the whole thing written out. It looked like this:

globe7februaryrichardiikillbeagleatthesewordswithmine ownbreathreleasealldutysriteskilldeliverer ofthismessage

Chapter 24

With Mine Own Breath

Tom went through the decoded message slowly, prising out the individual words from the mass of characters and adding punctuation where it seemed necessary. This was what he came up with:

> Globe, 7 February, Richard II, kill Beagle at these words: With mine own breath release all duty's rites. Kill deliverer of this message.

Alice listened almost disbelievingly as Tom read this out. Until now, she hadn't fully believed that the scribbled note she'd found in the chest under Richard's bed really did connect with the plot they'd uncovered at Essex House. It was just a fanciful theory – a way of keeping her hopes up that she might one day find her brother, or at least find out what had happened to him. Now, incredibly, the fanciful theory turned out to be true – Richard had indeed become mixed up in the plot. Someone, probably Gus, had given this message to Richard to deliver. Richard must have made a copy of it and placed it in the chest under his bed, before delivering the original to someone unknown.

Then came the last five words, and they hit her like a stone. *Kill deliverer of this message*. Without realising it, Richard had given the order for his own execution. Something seemed to collapse within Alice at this thought. She gripped the edges of the table, trying to prevent herself from sinking into a mire of despair.

The locket – remember the locket! It had been dry when she found it. Maybe he survived.

The killer dropped it there, said a cold, dreadful voice inside her head.

Tom noticed her misery and placed a hand on her arm. 'It may not be what you think,' he said. 'We don't know if Richard delivered this. The message is here, isn't it? So he probably didn't.'

'Then where is he?' cried Alice.

'I don't know,' said Tom. 'But you have to keep believing that he's alive.'

She wiped her eyes and took a deep breath. Tom was right. She had to keep believing. With an effort, she returned her attention to the revealed message. 'It says here *kill beagle*. You told me that *Beagle* is the name they call Lord Cecil. Does that mean someone's going to kill him?'

Tom nodded. 'It looks that way. And it's going to happen here at the Globe, this afternoon. So whoever sent this message must have known the Beagle was going to be here.'

'Gus!' Alice slammed her fist on the table. 'That was why he invited Cecil to come to this performance – he brought him here to be killed!'

They stared at each other. Alice thought about the clever arguments Gus had employed to lure Cecil here – his show of loyalty to the queen, his betrayal of his fellow conspirators – it had all been a pretence, all part of their devious plan.

The play had already begun – in fact it had been in progress for an hour or more. Alice strained her ears. If she listened hard, she could hear Richard Burbage, who was playing the king, delivering his lines on the stage, and, beyond that, the echoing murmur of the crowd. There were no panicked screams, no stampede of running feet – nothing to suggest a real murder had taken place. They weren't too late then. They could stop this. *But how?*

Tom was looking, once more, at the message. 'It says *Kill Beagle at these words: With mine own breath release all duty's rites*... What does that mean? *With mine own breath release all duty's rites*.'

'Who speaks my words?' said a voice nearby. They both looked up in time to see Will Shakespeare entering the room. He was accompanied by another of the company's sharers, John Heminges.

'Aha,' said Will, spotting Tom, 'it is my liberator from Hell.' He turned to Heminges. 'This is the boy I was telling you about, John, the one who thought Gus really died as Polonius.'

'We all thought Gus died as Polonius,' said John, and both men laughed.

'Just now I heard you say some words,' Will said to Tom. 'You said: *With mine own breath release all duty's rites*.'

'Are they... *your* words, Mr Shakespeare?' asked Tom.

'They most certainly are – they're from the dethronement scene in *Richard II* – the scene Gus insisted we include in this afternoon's production. They should be performing it at any moment.'

'Then we haven't much time,' said Alice, rising to her feet.

'Much time? Much time for what?' asked John.

Alice decided to come clean. Praying that John Heminges wasn't part of the conspiracy, she said: 'We believe we have uncovered a plot to murder the chief minister.'

'What?!'

John looked genuinely shocked – and she knew, from experience, that he wasn't that good a player. Feeling she could trust him, Alice showed John the deciphered message. He peered at it uncomprehendingly, so she read it to him.

'Who is this Beagle?' asked John when she'd finished.

'It's a nickname for the chief minister, commonly used by his enemies,' said Tom.

'Where did you get this?' John demanded, flapping the paper.

'It was among Richard's possessions,' Alice explained. 'I think... I think he delivered this message to the assassin. I'm sorry, but it seems Mr Phillips is involved in the plot.'

'Gus Phillips?!' John Heminges had by now grown very red-faced.

Alice nodded. 'Earlier this week, he secretly met with the chief minister's enemies, Lord Monteagle and Sir Gelly Meyrick, and then yesterday he invited the chief minister here.'

'How do you know all this, Adam?' asked John.

'I've been looking for my brother – trying to find out what happened to him. That led me to uncover this plot. Tom has been helping me...'

John turned to Will, who raised his eyebrows and said: 'Who can ever see into a man's heart? Even so, this is *Gus* we're talking about! I find it hard to picture him as an assassin.'

'He doesn't exactly have that "lean and hungry look",' agreed John.

Alice recognized this from Will's play, *Julius Caesar*. It was how Caesar described Cassius, one of the leaders of the plot to assassinate him.

'That line,' said John, '*With mine own breath release all*

duty's rites. It is, perhaps, the most incendiary line in the play – the moment when the king surrenders his power. Imagine it: just as Burbage utters these words, the queen's most powerful minister is killed in front of everybody. This could lead to chaos, cataclysm, civil war!'

'Which is exactly what they want,' said Alice.

'Hush,' said Will. He opened the door and cocked his head, listening carefully.

Alice could hear the words now being spoken by Richard Burbage: 'Alack, why am I sent for to a king, before I have shook off the regal thoughts wherewith I reign'd?'

'The dethronement scene has begun,' said Will. 'In just fifty more lines, the assassin will strike.'

'We can't let it happen!' cried John.

'Aye, we cannot!' said Will. 'My words might die upon the ear on occasion, but I never want it said they caused the death of any man.'

'We should stop the play,' said John.

'The killer might just as easily strike in the confusion that follows,' Will pointed out.

'We could warn Cecil,' suggested Alice.

'Agreed,' nodded John. 'I will go there now.' He moved towards the door.

'Wait!'

Everyone turned to see Tom. His sword was drawn and pointing at John Heminges. 'Don't move!' he said.

'Tom!' cried Alice. 'What are you doing?'

Chapter 25

A Visit to Heaven

Tom looked desperate. He could barely meet Alice's eyes. 'I'm sorry,' he said, 'but Lord Cecil is my master's enemy. It is right that he should die.'

'So now you're siding with the murderers of my brother,' said Alice, coating every word with disdain.

'It's not that simple,' said Tom. 'You don't know what's been happening. Cecil has poisoned the queen's mind against my master.' He was breathing hard, struggling to find the words he needed to convince them. 'The Earl of Essex is an honourable man – a hero! For years, he served his country and his queen with selfless devotion. All he wants is the chance to continue that life of service. But Cecil is bent on destroying him.'

'No, Tom, you're wrong about that,' said John. 'I don't know what they've been telling you over there at Essex House, but the truth is Essex is a dangerous, unstable hot-head. The queen knows that – she doesn't need to hear it from Cecil. Essex may tell you he's a great warrior, but he's lost more battles than he's won, and spilled far too much English blood in the process.'

'That's not true!' cried Tom, pushing the tip of his sword closer to John's throat. 'What about Cadiz? He took it single-handedly from the Spanish!'

'Is that what he told you?' laughed John. 'Then I don't suppose he mentioned the other commanders who helped him capture that city – Sir Walter Raleigh, Sir Francis Vere and Sir John Wingfield? Nor, I suppose, did he admit what a meaningless victory it was in the end – how quickly Cadiz was recaptured by the Spanish, and how angry the queen was when he failed to bring back any Spanish gold. From your face, I assume he didn't. In that case, you probably won't have heard of his disastrous expedition to the Azores in 1597, when he defied the queen's orders and took off after the Spanish treasure fleet without first defeating their battle fleet, very nearly leading to a Spanish invasion of England.'

Alice felt as though she was about to explode with frustration. 'Enough of this!' she cried. 'There's a man out there who killed my brother – and now he's about to kill again! You can't stop me, Tom. I'm going after him!' She made a dash for the door, but a powerful shove from Tom knocked her to the ground.

His eyes were wild as he stared down at her. They blazed with a frightened kind of anger. 'Don't you try to leave here! Any of you!' The tip of his sword roved around the room menacingly. Finally, it landed in front of John Heminge's chest. 'My master is a hero,' he told him. 'The queen loved him once, before Cecil got to her. And it sounds like Cecil's got to you, too, with his poisonous lies!'

'I have no love for Cecil,' said John. 'I've never even met the man. But I read the broadsides, and I've spoken to the veterans who've lost comrades – and *limbs* – following the reckless earl around the battlefields of France, the Low Countries and Ireland...'

'The men at Essex House love him – all former soldiers,' asserted Tom.

'Aye, I've heard he's generous with his knighthoods,' said John with a cynical sneer. 'It's remarkable how easy it is to make someone love you by giving them a title.'

'They'd die for him,' whispered Tom.

'As will Lord Cecil, in just one moment,' said Will. 'The speech is about to commence.'

'Think about who you're serving, Tom, and who you're betraying,' said John. 'Who do you love more – your master or your country? Are you an Englishman, or an Essex man? Will you live as a hero, or die a traitor, along with all the other idiots who choose to follow the power-crazed earl on his doomed insurrection?'

'I'm leaving!' said Alice, rising to her feet. She glowered

at Tom, hoping he could see all the contempt she felt for him right then. 'Strike me down if you want to,' she said to him. 'I'm going through that door right now!'

She waited for another blow from his fist or the cut of his cold steel blade as she marched out. None came.

In the Tiring-House, she could hear Burbage's words sounding clearly from the stage. He was surrendering his kingly regalia…

Now mark me, how I will undo myself;
I give this heavy weight from off my head
And this unwieldy sceptre from my hand…

These words were received by the audience with absolute silence. None there could have witnessed, or expected to witness, the voluntary abdication of a monarch being played out on a public stage.

Burbage was just a few short lines away from delivering the assassin's cue. Even now, the killer would be creeping towards his target, Lord Cecil, knife at the ready. She would have to act fast.

Alice knew the layout of the Globe better than anyone, having spent many an hour lurking behind, above and beneath the stage, delivering sound and visual effects for the plays. She realised she would not be able to reach the assassin in time. Her entry to the Lords Rooms – the area behind the stage where the nobles and courtiers sat – would be blocked by the personal guards of those seated on the balcony. But she could get to the Heavens – the room directly above the stage. From the trapdoor entrance in the floor of the Heavens, she would have a clear view of the Lords Rooms. She could shout or throw something at the killer – try to distract him, and at the same time alert the guards to his presence.

With this plan in mind, she departed the Tiring-House through an arched entrance and raced up a set of spiral wooden steps, taking three at a time. Within seconds she had reached the top step. From here, with practised agility, she dived into the Heavens. It was not, by any description, a heavenly kind of place – just a cramped, triangular room within the pitched roof that surmounted the stage. A small window at the far end admitted some light. The room was a jumble of special effects equipment. There was the thunder machine – a cannon ball in a wooden box on top of a see-saw; a pile of firecrackers – rolls of thick paper filled with gunpowder – for lightning; and a rope harness to allow players to descend to the stage through the trapdoor. There was even a small cannon near the window used for battle scenes.

Taking care not to stumble over any of this paraphernalia, Alice picked her way over to the trapdoor in the middle of the room and pulled it open. Directly below her stood Richard Burbage, solemnly renouncing his throne:

With mine own tears I wash away my balm…

Surrounding Burbage were several other players, including Edmund. Above them, on the balcony of the Lords Rooms, Alice observed the fascinated, frightened faces of the nobles and courtiers. They could scarcely believe the scene unfolding before them. Would they be blamed for having been here? Would they be banished from court?

With mine own hands I give away my crown...

In the midst of them sat Lord Cecil, a thin smile at play upon his lips. He alone had been expecting this, and was probably even now rehearsing to himself how he would describe it later to the queen.

He sat surrounded by his fellow courtiers. There was no sign of any assassin. Alice sat back on her heels. Had they been mistaken?

With mine own tongue deny my sacred state...

Then she saw something stirring in the shadows at the back of the balcony. A tall, slightly bent figure emerged from behind a curtain. He wore a monk-like cowl that obscured his face. One of his hands was tucked into the folds of his robe. As the figure edged closer to Cecil, his hand came into view. Something glinted there – *a knife!*

The assassin!

This was the man who had most likely killed Richard

– the last to see him alive. She wanted to kill him – but before that, she needed to hear from him what had happened. Alice wished she could swoop down in the harness and capture him, then force him to tell her everything. But there was no time for that. Instead, she drew a breath, preparing to scream out a warning to Cecil. Before she could, everything stopped. The murderer stopped advancing towards Cecil, the crowd stopped moving, and Burbage stopped speaking. Alice glanced towards the stage, wondering why he wasn't delivering the fateful line. She was surprised to see that the players had been joined by another figure who had entered unexpectedly from the Tiring-House.

It was Tom!

Her heart beat faster. What was *he* doing there?

His appearance on stage should not, in itself, have prevented Burbage from continuing with his performance. He was a seasoned player, after all, and had experienced stage invasions in the past. What had rendered him speechless – and the sight of this shocked Alice as much as everyone else in the playhouse – was Tom's sword, which was pointing at Burbage's chest. At the same time, Tom had placed a finger to his lips. In other words: *Be quiet, or die!*

The audience, having fallen into a brief, stunned silence, was now roused to anger at this interloper, who was threatening their favourite player *and* spoiling a tense and dramatic scene. Someone shouted that the trespasser was a censor from the Revels Office, and this inflamed the crowd even more. The wealthy citizens in the galleries jeered and catcalled, and the groundlings hissed and spat their fury like a pit of frenzied snakes.

With such a noise filling the theatre, Alice could have screamed at the top of her lungs that a killer was about to strike, and still she would not have been heard. Fortunately, the assassin continued to hesitate. His cue line had not been uttered. The knife disappeared back inside his robe.

More incensed than anyone in the audience was a large man in one of the galleries adjacent to the Lords Rooms. He was on his feet, leaning over the wooden rail and screaming at Tom, his plump red face glistening with sweat. Alice recognised him as Sir Gelly, one of the conspirators.

As she watched, she saw him raise his eyes to the Lords Rooms and stare hard at the monk-like figure behind Lord Cecil. The killer met his gaze, and Sir Gelly gave a firm nod.

Alice could guess what this meant. Sir Gelly was ordering him to proceed with the murder in spite of Tom's intervention. Since she could do nothing to stop this with her voice, she looked around for something to throw. Her eyes lit on the box of firecrackers.

Chapter 26

Balcony Fight

On the stage, Tom was being pelted with nutshells, apple cores, shoes and other assorted objects by angry groundlings. He retreated towards the rear of the stage as he attempted to deflect the barrage with his arms and his sword. A big, wet, rotten-smelling tomato slammed against his cheek. He managed to slice a cabbage in two just before it hurtled into him, but was unable to prevent a leather ale bottle colliding painfully with his shoulder.

What have I done? he asked himself. *What was I thinking of?*

It certainly wasn't John Heminges who had persuaded him to step out here. There may have been some truth in what Heminges had said about his master – who could be sure? But Heminges could have called the earl a murderer of children, and it wouldn't have swayed Tom one jot. What had swayed him, in the end, was Adam and that look he'd given him just before he stormed out. Tom could not abide the thought of being so hated by his friend. Why that should be, he did not know. They had been acquainted only a few days, and yet he felt a powerful need to please him. It had driven him to help Adam that day at Essex House, and willingly endure the beatings that followed, and now it drove him onto this stage with barely a thought for the consequences.

As he fell back towards the Tiring-House, Tom spied Sir Gelly directly above him. His face was as shiny and pink as an apple as he hurled abuse at him from the gallery next to the Lords Rooms. Two thoughts flashed into Tom's head at this sight: the first was that he had gone too far this time – he had burned his bridges with Essex House and could never go back; the second was that he didn't care.

Then he saw Sir Gelly lift his head and nod at someone on the balcony. Tom guessed this was the killer. So Sir Gelly was proceeding with the assassination without the cue line, perhaps gambling that the audience had already been sufficiently roused to rebellion.

Tom knew he had to stop the assassination. Fate, or Adam, had forced him into this role of saving the hateful Lord Cecil. But how could he get up there? Still under fire from the groundlings, he looked around and spied the pillars that supported the balcony. Without thinking, he leapt onto one of these and began a desperate climb towards the Lords Rooms. The wooden pillar was painted to look like pink marble, and it had a marble-like slipperiness that made it hard for Tom to maintain a grip. The curses of the hostile crowd filled his ears. He was getting peppered with nutshells, and a putrid orange exploded against his head. Someone behind him pulled at his cloak, and he began sliding downwards. He squeezed the column with all his might to arrest his fall. Kicking backwards, his foot connected with something soft and he heard a groan. His arms burned, but he forced his way through the pain and continued up the pillar, inch by agonising inch. Finally, he managed to slap a hand against the base of the balustrade that formed the balcony's edge. Squeezing the last drop of energy from his body, he placed his other hand next to it, then swung his foot upwards. It caught between two balusters and wedged there.

At the same time, he felt a painful kick to his chest. He looked up to see that he was under assault from a courtier on the balcony – quite a weedy-looking fellow, fortunately. Using one of the balusters for leverage, Tom hauled himself to his feet. He knocked the nobleman aside and leapt over the balustrade. Other courtiers were now on their feet, backing away from him, and Tom was vaguely aware that he must appear quite a frightening figure, drenched in sweat and swinging his sword. Armed guards were surging through the curtain at the back, knocking over chairs to reach him. Lord Cecil, dressed in his customary black, was on the far side of the central, projecting balcony, some ten feet from where Tom stood.

He, too, was on his feet, head thrust forward, scowling at Tom. Right behind the chief minister, and standing almost a foot taller, was a man dressed in a hooded cloak. The hood completely covered his head, obscuring his face. Everyone's eyes were on Tom, so no one saw the man raising his hand or the long knife clutched in his fist.

Tom saw it, though, and saw, too, that he was too late. He couldn't reach Cecil or the assassin in time – there were too many people in the way. So he scrambled up onto the top of the balustrade. The perch was narrow and precarious, and the drop to the stage from this height could easily have been fatal, but Tom didn't think about that. He skipped forwards along the slender parapet, just evading the groping hands of the guards attempting to catch him, and then he dived – straight at Cecil.

There was a scream of scraping chair legs, the swish of a knife blade and a flailing of thin, bony limbs. The next thing Tom knew, he was on the floor of the balcony with his face pressed into the chief minister's lace ruff. He twisted himself free of Cecil and looked up in time to see the hooded figure, now on his knees, raising his knife for the second time.

Before he could stab Cecil, the killer's body was

rocked by a huge bang as an eye-searing flash flew down from the painted ceiling above them. It sparkled and burned through the air and landed on the balcony inches from the killer. The assassin lurched backwards and collapsed against the balustrade, groaning for breath as if he'd been winded.

Tom glanced upwards, wondering what in heaven he had just witnessed. There, crouched over an open trapdoor in the middle of the painted ceiling, was Adam. He waved at him. Somewhat stunned, Tom waved back.

Meanwhile, the four guards who had been after Tom hastily reassessed the situation and now turned their swords on the assassin. 'Put down the knife!' one of them screamed at him.

The assassin ignored them. The sound of his breathing was terrible – like a slow, wheezing death.

'Back away from Mr Scrope, if you value your life!' bellowed someone from the far end of the balcony.

Tom's head jerked up at the sound of this familiar Welsh intonation. Sir Gelly had arrived and was swinging his sword above his head like some pirate of the high seas – he must have leapt across the gap between the gallery and the Lords Rooms balcony. Behind him were half a dozen mercenaries from Essex House. The balcony was otherwise deserted, the courtiers all having fled, leaving a lot of overturned velvet-seated chairs.

The guards immediately turned on the newcomers

and began to fight them. Soon the air clattered and rang with the sound of colliding sword blades.

'I'm coming for you, Tom,' screamed Sir Gelly, as he duelled with one of the guards. 'I'm going to kill you for what you did today.'

Tom tightened his grip on his sword. He would be ready for him this time.

Below the balcony, the stage was by now empty, and a violent fight had broken out among the groundlings in the yard. As for the galleries, they were fast emptying of spectators.

'Thank you, young sir, for saving my life,' said a frail voice near Tom's elbow.

He turned to see Lord Cecil still lying there next to him, his hair awry and a red mark on his cheek but otherwise unharmed.

Tom nodded coldly. He hadn't done any of this for the Beagle. He got to his feet, then helped Cecil up.

'You should get away from here,' he advised him.

'You, too,' said Cecil. 'From the sound of it, Sir Gelly Meyrick wants your blood.'

Tom watched Cecil leave, but did not follow him. He had decided to stay and help the guards in their struggle with Sir Gelly and his rebels. As he moved to join the fight, he heard Adam yelling at him from above:

'Get him! Get the killer!'

Tom whirled around. The hooded man was no longer lying sprawled against the balustrade, but was now moving at speed towards the curtain at the back of the balcony. He hadn't given up on killing Cecil.

Before the assassin could reach the curtain, it swished aside. Tom hoped it might be fresh guards arriving. Instead, he was surprised to see Edmund Squires – Adam's friend – bounding onto the balcony, still dressed in his stage costume.

'Stop that man!' Tom yelled at Edmund. 'He's the assassin!'

But Edmund did not stop him. Instead, to Tom's complete bewilderment, he held the curtain aside for him. 'There you go, Mr Scrope,' said Edmund, ushering him through.

'What did you do that for?' yelled Tom.

'Because his work is not complete,' Edmund replied with an amiable smile. 'We paid him to kill Lord Cecil, and now he must do so.'

Tom tried to charge after the killer, but Edmund blocked his way. He swung his sword at Tom, who had to quickly spin aside to avoid losing an arm.

What was going on? Edmund was supposed to be Adam's friend!

With no time to ponder why Edmund was attacking him, Tom raised his own weapon and retaliated with a horizontal cut aimed at his left shoulder. Edmund, still smiling, parried with a vertical sword. The smile turned malicious, and the parry became a thrust as he forced his sword down and forwards. Tom was obliged to retreat. Edmund came at him again, aiming blows towards his head and neck, first from one side and then the other. Desperately, Tom blocked and parried. His opponent was quick – quicker than Sir Gelly. Tom tried to remember what Sir John had taught him – about posture, balance and grip – but it was hard to consider such things when someone was attacking you so ferociously and from so many different angles. With no time to think, he fought on pure instinct, living from second to second, aware that the smallest slip could mean death or horrible mutilation.

As he frantically fought off his attacker, Tom was being driven steadily backwards, ever closer to the balustrade. Soon he was pressed right up against it, and Edmund, sensing victory, redoubled his attacks. He brought his sword arm down in a vicious cut towards Tom's forehead. Sparks flew as Tom blocked it, and the terrific force of the blow sent shockwaves of pain through his arm and shoulder. He was tiring now. Edmund knew this and continued to press downwards. Their blades slid against each other until both swords became locked together at the hilts. Tom felt himself toppling backwards as Edmund tried to force him over the balcony. 'Die, traitor!' cried Edmund.

Traitor?

'Kill him, Edmund!' boomed Sir Gelly. He was standing nearby, cheering him on, having dispatched his own opponent. The balcony, it seemed, was now in the hands of the rebels.

Tom was exhausted. Through blurry eyes, he took in Edmund's manic grin, the bulging muscles in his neck, the vein throbbing in his temple. He couldn't fight him any longer. He was falling…

But then a bird, or something like it, came swooping out of the sky. There was a loud thump, and Edmund collapsed to the ground. Tom, who was still teetering on the edge of the parapet, had to grab the balustrade with both hands to stop himself from falling right over. After hauling himself to safety, he looked up to see Adam standing on the balcony looking down at Edmund, who was now on the floor, clutching his head and groaning with pain. Adam was in a harness, with ropes around him stretching up to the trapdoor in the ceiling. He must have flown down from there and delivered an almighty kick to Edmund.

Sir Gelly advanced angrily on Adam as he hastily detached himself from his harness, but before Sir Gelly and his soldiers had moved three paces, there came a thunderstorm of approaching bootsteps, and a dozen armed yeomen guards charged through the curtains. Seeing this, Sir Gelly fled across the balcony and took a death-defying leap back to the gallery he had arrived from. He landed with a stumbling crash, knocking over several chairs, before escaping through a doorway. After a short scuffle, the remaining rebels, along with Edmund, were overpowered and placed under arrest.

'Why, Edmund?' Adam wanted to know as a yeoman shackled his wrists.

The young man was no longer smiling. As his eyes

met Adam's they glittered with a defiant kind of pride. 'I was doing my duty to the Earl of Essex,' he said, '– the man who, God willing, will be our next king.'

Adam gaped at him, mouth open. 'What about Richard?' he whispered. 'And the message. Was it… you?'

'Aye,' he said, as the guard hauled him towards the balcony exit. 'I had your brother killed. Couldn't keep him alive, could I? Or he'd have ratted on us, given the whole thing away.'

As Edmund was pushed through the curtain, Adam ran after him, with Tom following close behind.

'I hope they kill you for this, Edmund!' Adam screamed at him from the top of the steps as he was led towards the ground floor.

Edmund twisted his head to catch Adam's eye. The anger was gone from his face now. 'Richard did it to protect you,' he said to him.

'What do you mean?' demanded Adam.

'I told him I'd reveal your secret if he didn't deliver the message to Scrope.'

'What sec–?' Adam stopped, and placed his hands over his reddening cheeks. Tom looked at him, puzzled.

Edmund smirked at them as the guards pulled him off the staircase, around a corner and out of sight. His final shout echoed in their ears: 'I always knew you were a girl, Alice!'

Chapter 27

River Walk

Alice's mind was reeling. She couldn't believe that Edmund, her best friend, had sent Richard to be killed. He'd used blackmail to force him to deliver that message.

'Richard did it for me,' she whispered. 'He did it to protect me.'

She felt Tom's hand upon her arm. 'We don't know for sure if he was killed,' he said.

'Only one man knows that, and that's the killer,' said Alice. 'Come on!' She began running down the stairs, almost tripping in her haste.

On the street outside the Globe, they found a small crowd had congregated like carrion crows at a battlefield. The mercenaries from Essex House, whose job had been to stir up the mob after Cecil's murder, had fled or been captured. This crowd was made up of ordinary members of the public – locals and playgoers. They were gathered around something. To judge from their expressions, it was quite gruesome.

Shouldering their way through the throng, Alice and Tom came upon the object of everyone's interest: the mysterious Mr Scrope was lying there, quite still, in a pool of blood.

'The guards must have got him – hopefully before he got Cecil,' muttered Tom.

Alice reached down and pulled back Scrope's hood.

There was a collective groan from the crowd as they took in his appearance, which was severely disfigured as if from some disease. His dome of a bald head was lumpy and misshapen. One eye bulged unnaturally. His nose was so swollen that it pressed down upon his mouth, forcing his lips into a permanent sneer.

Alice closed her eyes – not from revulsion, but from crushing disappointment, because Mr Scrope, the last man to see Richard alive, was unquestionably dead.

Guards arrived and ordered the crowd to disperse. Scrope's body was dumped onto a cart and taken away. Alice, feeling dazed by the afternoon's events, allowed Tom to guide her away from the scene. The two of them began to wander side by side along the river bank.

'Thank you,' said Tom, 'for dropping out of Heaven like that. You saved my life.'

'You were brave,' said Alice. 'I couldn't believe it when I saw you on the stage, and then climbing up that pillar and diving on Scrope... Was it what Mr Heminges said that finally convinced you?'

Tom shook his head. 'No, it was you – that look you gave me.'

'What look?'

'Just before you stormed out. You seemed full of hate.'

'I *was* – at that moment.'

'I couldn't bear it.'

He looked distraught at the memory. Alice was surprised. She had no idea that he even cared what she thought of him. She felt a flutter of pleasure at this revelation. But it was only a very small thing next to the vastness of her unhappiness, like the garden of Essex House surrounded by all the slums of London.

'Is it true, what Edmund said?' Tom asked.

'Aye,' she said quietly. 'I'm a girl. My name is Alice.'

Tom stopped walking. She turned to him, trying to interpret his frown. *Was he angry?*

'I'm sorry,' she said. 'I know you guessed earlier, and I know I lied, but I had no choice.'

'You could have trusted me,' he said.

'The fewer who know, the better. See what Edmund did once he found out. He forced Richard to...'

She continued walking along the path, so that Tom wouldn't see her sob.

Hearing his footsteps hurrying to catch up with her, she walked faster.

'Wait!' he said, and he tried to grab her hand, but she pulled it away. She didn't want his or anyone's comfort. Her secret was to blame for her brother's death. Richard had been trying to protect her… This thought was too painful for words. She felt a terrible pressure in her chest, as if her heart was going to explode. In that moment, she wished she could die. She could hear the watermen crying out their prices for upstream and down. What price would they give to take her to the bottom of the river?

And then, suddenly, she stopped walking. They had reached a set of stone steps leading down to a jetty. This was the place where, four days earlier, Alice had come with Edmund. She recognised it, although yellow-green water now rocked and swirled over the muddy beach where she'd found the locket. Unconsciously she reached for it beneath her tunic, caressing its engraved surface.

'You mustn't blame yourself,' said Tom.

She glanced at him. He was nervous, unsure of what to say to her, but his eyes were kind. He meant well.

'This was where I found Richard's locket,' she said, showing him the ornament around her neck. 'The tide was out. I saw it on the beach.'

'You said it was dry when you found it,' said Tom.

'It was. At first I thought that Richard dropped it there. I thought it was proof that he was alive. But then I realised that it could just as easily have been tossed there by the killer. Or by…' She stopped as a more uncomfortable thought struck her. 'Or by Edmund!'

'Edmund?'

'He was with me that day.' She frowned, trying to recall the exact moments leading up to the discovery. 'I was distracted, I remember, by a fancy-looking barge heading down the river. While I was looking at that, he must have… he must have thrown it down onto the sand.'

'How did Edmund get hold of it?'

'He probably stole it from Richard.'

'But why did he throw it onto the sand?'

'Because he wanted me to find it. I remember now, he was trying to talk me out of going to Essex House. He was probably worried I'd uncover the plot. So he threw the locket down there, hoping I'd see it and think that Richard had drowned, so I'd give up on my quest. I nearly did. I broke down in tears when I saw it, and after that he left, assuming I'd go back home. But then I saw the locket was dry, and that gave me fresh hope.' She grimaced. 'For a few days, at least!'

'Don't lose that hope,' said Tom. 'You never know, your brother may still be alive.'

She sniffed and attempted a smile. 'Thank you, Tom,' she said, not really persuaded, but appreciating the comment. 'Do you… Do you still want to be my friend, even though I'm not a boy?'

Tom knitted his brows, and she could see he was pretending to give the matter a great deal of thought. Then he grinned. 'I'd be honoured,' he said.

'Just remember to keep calling me *Adam* in public,'

she warned.

'I'll try to remember... It must be hard though, I mean for *you* – having to be a boy all the time. How do you manage?'

'I've been doing it for so long now, it's become a habit,' she said. 'Sometimes, I almost feel like I am a boy.' She paused, smiling at his confusion. 'I wouldn't expect you to understand.'

Tom was about to respond, but she hushed him with a look. Over his shoulder, she'd seen two familiar figures rapidly approaching.

Gus Phillips and John Heminges stopped when they saw her.

'Adam!' cried Gus. 'We've been looking everywhere for you! We're wanted at the palace – summoned by Lord Cecil. He survived, by the way, thanks almost entirely to your efforts.'

'And Tom's,' said Alice, indicating her friend.

'Of course!' said Gus. 'Thank you, young man.'

'I'm glad you came to your senses, Tom,' said John. 'That was quite extraordinary what you did, confronting the killer like that.'

'Your arguments were most persuasive!' said Tom, giving Alice a surreptitious wink.

Chapter 28
The Englishman

It was evening by the time the four of them set out in a canopied barge across the Thames towards Whitehall Palace. The sun was sinking over Charing Cross, and the placid river was like a highway of beaten gold upon which, here and there, drifted the lonely silhouettes of wherry-boats. The wharves and quays of the north bank were so dense with the masts of ships moored there for the night, they appeared like wooded groves.

Soon enough, the imposing white stone frontage of the palace appeared on their right, illuminated by hundreds of torches. The forecourt was full of heavily armed guards. Lord Cecil was clearly taking the threat from Essex House very seriously. The visitors were led at lightning pace through the courtyard and the maze-like interior of the palace. Tom couldn't help gawping in wonder at the luxury, grandeur and exoticism on display. Alice, of course, had seen it all before.

Finally, they arrived in Lord Cecil's study, which, in contrast to the rest of the building, was conspicuously gloomy and austere. It was also cold – for Cecil insisted on admitting the chill February air through an open casement.

The chief minister did not seem ruffled by his close shave with death just a few hours earlier. He was relaxed and even courteous as he showed his guests to their seats. Nevertheless, Tom noted how his gaze kept returning to Gus Phillips.

'It is a blessing to us all – indeed the entire nation – that you are still with us, your grace,' said John. 'May I take this opportunity to apologise on behalf of the Chamberlain's Men for this calamitous incident. I do hope it won't dissuade you from future visits to our playhouse.'

'Aye, well, I wouldn't hold your breath about that,' harrumphed Cecil. He turned to Tom and Alice. 'I want to thank you two for saving my life today. Had it not been for your prompt and decisive action, I would most certainly not be sitting here before you now.'

Tom lowered his eyes on hearing this. The chief minister could have no idea how close he'd come to siding with the rebels. It seemed strange to think of it now. True, he felt no personal warmth towards Lord

Cecil, and despised his treatment of his master, but the man was chief minister to the queen of England. Attacking him was in some ways like attacking the country! It wasn't only Alice's look of hate that had brought Tom to his senses. If he was honest, there was also something in his gut that had recoiled against the whole idea of killing Cecil. John Heminges had asked him if he was an Englishman or an Essex man. Today, Tom discovered that he was an Englishman.

'We have extracted confessions from Edmund Squires and two others we managed to capture today,' Cecil continued. 'From what they told us, it seems that Sir Gelly and Lord Monteagle had laid plans for a carefully coordinated sequence of events this afternoon. Sir Gelly had planted a number of soldiers among the crowd. The plan was that when a certain line was spoken by Richard Burbage, playing King Richard II, this would act as the trigger both for the assassin to kill me, and for these hidden soldiers to lead a "spontaneous" uprising in support of the Earl of Essex in the playhouse. As Sir Gelly imagined it, this uprising would spread beyond the Globe into the surrounding streets and, ultimately, right across the city. At this vulnerable moment, with the royal guard, the city marshal and all his constables distracted by the disorder, the Earl of Essex would strike. He would ride along the Strand and into Whitehall, gathering eager followers as he went, and lead an attack on the palace.

'It was not an entirely unrealistic plan, for we all know what a popular fellow the earl is. He might have pulled it off – which is why your intervention, Tom, was so crucial. By preventing Burbage from speaking that line, not only did you cause the assassin to hesitate, you also sowed confusion among the soldiers who were expecting to hear it. Their uprising became, instead, a chaotic brawl that the guards were easily able to subdue.'

At this point, Lord Cecil's eye fell upon Gus Phillips, and his demeanour became noticeably chillier. 'All of which,' he said, 'brings us to *your* role in the day's events, Mr Phillips.' As he said this, Tom noticed the guards at the door moving several steps closer to the back of Gus's chair. Despite the chill in the room, several beads of sweat now appeared on the dome of Gus's high forehead.

'It was you who met Sir Gelly and Lord Monteagle, was it not?' said Cecil. 'And then you came here yesterday and told me all about it – out of a sense of loyalty, you said.'

'Indeed I did, sire,' said Gus, nodding with a desperate kind of eagerness.

'Come to the Globe, you said, and make sure you come *alone*, without any troops. It sounds to me, Mr Phillips, that you lured me into a trap!'

Gus had turned unhealthily pale, almost grey. 'Sire, I assure you,' he blustered, 'I meant every word. I have been *used* – grossly and hideously *used*.... I spoke the truth to you yesterday in every respect but one, which was this: it was Lord Monteagle who told me to invite you to the Globe.'

'What!' cried Cecil, rising to his feet with such ferocity it sent his chair tumbling.

Gus quailed. 'It happened after the meeting, sire. Lord Monteagle stopped me in the courtyard as I was leaving Essex House. He confided to me that Sir Gelly had gone too far this time and he wanted no part in this plot. He had pretended to go along with it, nay even encourage it, because he hoped the plot would prove the undoing of the Earl of Essex and his band of rebels. Monteagle advised me to come here to the palace and disclose to you all the details of the plan. He said I should even invite you to the Globe so that you could see for yourself the extent of the earl's treachery and convey this to the queen. He seemed genuine, sire. He looked so exhausted and fearful. Of course I had no idea that all this was just a ruse, that I was being manipulated. Sire, you have to believe me! I was shocked to the core when that man attacked you!'

'Why didn't you tell me that Lord Monteagle had said this?' Cecil demanded. 'Why did you include him as a conspirator, along with Sir Gelly?'

'He told me to, sire. He said you hated him and wanted nothing more than to see his head roll. He said that if you knew he was part of the plot, you would be more likely to take it seriously. He assured me it didn't matter to him, for he was going abroad for a while to lie low. Now I realise that it didn't matter to him because… because by this time, he assumed you would be...'

'Dead?' prompted Lord Cecil.

'I-Indeed, sire.'

Cecil stared at Gus in cold silence for a very long time. Finally, his thin lips cracked in an unexpected smile. 'I was testing you, Mr Phillips. I knew you were innocent all along. Edmund Squires, who has no love for you, told us that you were never a part of this plot.'

Gus looked almost ready to cry with relief as he dabbed his eyes and forehead with a handkerchief.

'Monteagle is as slippery as a snake,' added Cecil. 'And this is exactly the kind of trick he is known for. He flirts with rebellion, but never quite goes through with it, preferring to disappear at the last minute – which is why I have spent almost my entire career trying and failing to catch him.'

'We are most relieved, sire, that the plot was foiled and disaster averted,' said John Heminges. 'We will all rest easier in our beds tonight.'

'I am afraid there will be no rest tonight, Mr Heminges,' said Cecil. 'The danger is far from over. The ring-leader of today's attack, Sir Gelly Meyrick, escaped the scene. We must assume he is back at Essex House, along with his master, Essex, and their accomplices, Southampton, Rutland, Sussex, Bedford, Cromwell, Sandys and probably Monteagle. Tonight, Essex House is effectively enemy territory. The rebels have some two hundred well-armed men at their disposal. Even now, they are probably planning a new attack. We don't know when this will be or what form it will take. I wish I had an ear somewhere in that building...'

'I'll go!' volunteered Tom.

Everyone looked at him in surprise.

'Are you sure, Tom?' asked Cecil. 'You saw Sir Gelly today. He looked like he was ready to tear you limb from limb.'

Tom had never been so sure of anything in his life. This was his chance to make amends for his near-treachery.

'I know the layout of Essex House better than anyone,' he said. 'I can guess where they'll be meeting. I'm sure I'll be able to get you the information you need.'

'The house will be heavily fortified,' said Cecil. 'How do you plan to get past the guards on the wall?'

'I can help with that,' said Alice. She turned to Tom and he saw a faint smile crease her lips. 'Perhaps we could do this together, sire.'

Hearing her say this, Tom felt a pulse of disquiet. He didn't relish the thought of her risking her life. This was *his* fight!

'Adam,' began John, 'it's very brave of you to volunteer, but this is a highly dangerous enterprise and we need you at the Globe...'

'Mr Heminges is right,' said Tom firmly. 'I don't need you there, Adam. I can find a way in, I know I can.'

Her smile turned into an aggrieved pout.

Then Lord Cecil spoke: 'You'll need a partner,

Tom. Adam should go with you.'

Tom opened his mouth to object, but he could see from Cecil's expression that there was no point in arguing.

'England is indebted to both of you for your bravery in volunteering for this mission,' said Cecil. 'Because of the urgency of the crisis facing us, it's best if you leave at once. One of my barges will take you close to the river wall of Essex House. After that, you'll be on your own. Godspeed!'

Chapter 29

Firecracker

The barge sat low in the water. It was sleek and plain with none of the finery of the regal vessel that had conveyed them to the palace earlier. The two oarsmen steered the barge downriver, a single lantern hung near the prow guiding them through the misty darkness. The only sound was the splash of the oars. In the rear seat, Tom and Alice sat side by side in silence. She hadn't said a word to him since they'd left Cecil's study. He knew she was upset and that he ought to try and make it up to her – he just couldn't think what to say. Eventually, sick of the silence, he said: 'I'm sorry.'

'It's because I'm a girl, isn't it?' she murmured. 'That's why you don't want me here.'

'No.'

'I wish I'd never told you about that. I'm still Adam. I haven't changed. It's *you* who's changed.'

Was she right? Maybe. Still, it irritated him the way she thought she could read his heart. Defensively, he pushed the focus back onto her. 'Why do you even *want* to do this? This can't be about finding Richard…'

'I want to help you, that's why. You risked everything to help *me*, didn't you? That's what friends do.'

This took him aback. He'd never had a *friend* before. There were people he'd got on with at Essex House, but this felt different – more special. And that, he now realised, was part of the problem. He was starting to care a bit too much for Alice.

'I'm glad you're here,' he said after a moment's thought. 'I'm also worried. I don't like to think of what Sir Gelly will do to you if we get caught.'

'We won't get caught,' Alice replied. 'That's what I'm here for. I know how to avoid being seen and heard. Richard and I used to break into these sorts of places all the time for food. You just concentrate on *your* job, which is to get us to the right part of the house. I'll do the rest.'

'How are you going to get us into the grounds?' Tom asked.

'With this,' said Alice, pulling a small paper-covered cylinder out of her pocket.

'What's that?' asked Tom.

'A firecracker. It's used for lightning effects at the

Globe. I found it in the Heavens, and took it with me when I swooped down to save you. I thought it might come in handy – and it has!'

Tom's jaw fell open. 'You took an incendiary into Whitehall Palace?'

She nodded, grinning. 'All the way into Lord Cecil's private rooms! I could have completed Mr Scrope's mission, if I'd wanted to.'

'And tonight your job is to make sure we're not seen and heard, and you're planning to do that with a firecracker?'

'Aye.'

'How?'

'You'll see,' she smiled.

As they neared Essex House, they could see torches on the crenellated walls, reflected on metallic weapons and armour. The house was well defended, as if expecting a siege. Alice shuffled over to the oarsmen and pointed out a landing place on the north bank, close to their destination but screened from any watchers on the wall by a cluster of tall-masted boats. The men began to steer towards it, finding mooring space between two of these towering craft.

The oarsmen were a pair of powerfully built, middle-aged men with steel-grey beards and stony, deadpan faces. After securing the barge, they disembarked, along with Alice and Tom. The jetty led to some steps that took them up to Mylford Lane, which ran between

The Strand and the river and acted as a boundary between Essex House to the east and Arundel House to the west. The lane was quiet and very dark. Even so, Tom sensed that guards on the walls of Essex House were watching it very closely.

They concealed themselves behind a cart loaded up with barrels. Alice handed the firecracker to one of the oarsmen. The little cylinder ended in an inch-long twist of paper. This, she explained, was the fuse. She told him to count slowly to forty, then light it and toss it over the wall of Essex House. After that, he and his companion should race back to the barge and make their escape. So *that* was her plan – to use the firecracker as a diversion.

Tom told the oarsmen to remain in this part of the river and await their signal to be picked up. Then Alice motioned him to follow her. They moved swiftly in a semi-crouch towards the corner of Essex House where the riverside and Mylford Lane walls met. From here, they began to pick their way along the base of the river wall. The ledge was very narrow, and Tom found it hard to keep pace with the more sure-footed Alice. Black water lapped inches beneath his shoes – a cold, echoing, pitiless sound. He was uncomfortably aware that a single slip on the smooth, damp stone could send him tumbling in there. His fingers groped for and clung tight to every crack and crevice they could find in the brickwork. Above him, Tom could see the moon limned in orange torchlight. If a guard happened to peer down now, he would see them and everything would be over very quickly. Fire above, water below – what a place to find himself!

They were nearing the watergate when Alice stopped and twisted around to look at Tom. She was like a cat, he noticed – her body in perfect balance on its precarious perch. She whispered: 'It's been about forty seconds... When we hear that cracker, count to ten, then climb over this wall. Understood?'

'Aye.'

Tom raised his head and tried to mentally navigate his route up the wall, using the available foot and hand holds. It looked straightforward, but he wasn't a natural at this.

They waited.

Alice hissed her impatience.

And then they heard it: a loud crack. A flash of light lit up the sky above Mylford Lane, briefly silvering the river.

All along the wall, there were gasps and shouts. Tom heard footsteps moving away from them as the guards scurried off to investigate the explosion.

'Now!' cried Alice, and Tom scrambled upwards. His feet slipped as he tried to clamber over the battlements, but he managed to cling on with his arms. He swung helplessly from the top of the wall as his feet scrabbled to find purchase. Then he regained his footing, and vaulted over the top. As he did so, he collided forcefully with something that felt like a metal-plated bear.

Chapter 30

Palace, Tower or City?

Whatever it was staggered backwards beneath Tom's weight and momentum, and a deep voice let out a curse. Tom realised that he'd hurled himself directly into a guard! The heavy, armoured figure toppled backwards from the inner ledge of the wall, landing with a thump on the ground below.

Glancing to his right, Tom saw no one on the watergate. To his left, he glimpsed torches moving rapidly in the opposite direction. Luckily, the guard had been the only one left on the scene – and he seemed to have been rendered unconscious by the fall.

'Come on!' called Alice from below.

Tom leapt down, landing untidily on the grass. Rising to his feet, he dashed over to where she was waiting for him beneath a mulberry tree. From there they followed a zigzag course across the garden, scampering between various hiding-places – trees, statues, an arbour and a fountain – gradually progressing towards the house. Behind them they could hear guards still running around in confusion. Soon the guards would realise that the firecracker had been a diversion for something else and they would start searching for intruders.

Tom led Alice through a doorway into the servants' quarters. They darted down a passageway and into the buttery, which was thankfully empty. In the room's arched recesses stood several large barrels of wine and beer. Tom could hear chopping and pounding and raised voices coming from the kitchen next door – no doubt, meals were being prepared for the earl and his companions. Dare he show himself to the kitchen staff? They might have gleaned some valuable information about the earl's plans. Equally, they might have heard that he was now a traitor to the cause, and decide to turn him over to Sir Gelly. He decided he couldn't take the risk of revealing his presence to anyone.

'What now?' asked Alice. 'Do we go through the Great Hall like last time?'

Tom shook his head. 'No, we'll be spotted immediately. There's a staircase near here that will take us very close to the earl's private quarters. I often use it to bring him wine in the evenings. I'm sure that's where he'll be meeting with his friends.'

He opened the door very slightly so that he could peer out, then quickly closed it again. A couple of guards were standing near the back door. They must have come in from the garden. He could hear them walking up the passage, their footsteps ringing on the flagstones.

The kitchen sounds grew louder. A door must have been opened. Then he heard talking. A gruff voice: 'Keep your eyes peeled… There may be someone about…'

Tom and Alice waited for the footsteps to continue up the passageway, but they didn't. The guards had decided to remain where they were.

'We're stuck,' whispered Tom.

Then another, lighter set of footsteps approached. To Tom's alarm, the door to the buttery suddenly swung open. There was no time to hide. He pressed himself to the wall on one side of the doorway, and Alice did the same on the other, as Owen, the groom, came in. They watched him walk over to one of the barrels, turn a wooden tap at its base and start filling a jug with wine. He would see them when he turned around and then he'd yell out in surprise and the guards would come running. Tom couldn't let that happen.

In three quick strides, Tom ran up behind him. He clapped one hand over Owen's mouth while grabbing him around the middle with the other, pressing his arm to his side. Owen emitted a muffled scream and tried to twist around, swinging his free arm as if planning to strike his assailant with the wine jug. Wine spilled everywhere, including over Tom. It also continued to pour from the barrel, forming a purplish pool on the floor, until Alice ran over and closed the tap. Owen continued to struggle, but he was small of build and no match for Tom. He soon gave up and allowed himself to be pulled into one of the arched recesses. His eyes were wide and frightened as they stared into Tom's.

'It's okay,' Tom whispered to him. 'I'm not going to hurt you. Just promise me you won't make a sound.'

Owen nodded his assent to this, and Tom took his hand away from his mouth. The boy then immediately started gabbling: 'What's going on, Tom? Sir Gelly said you–'

Alice slapped him hard across the cheek, shocking both Owen and Tom. 'He told you to be quiet,' she whispered fiercely.

Owen stared at her, mouth wide open, hand pressed to his reddening cheek. Tom wondered what they could do with him. He hadn't planned on taking prisoners, but they couldn't very well release him either.

It was Alice who came up with a solution. She moved closer to Owen and whispered to him: 'There are soldiers surrounding this house. The siege will begin very soon. It's all over for your master. But you can survive this, if you do as you're told. Do you understand?'

The groom nodded slowly.

'Good. Now what I want you to do is go back out

there and have a word with those guards. Tell them that you've just remembered seeing Tom about five minutes ago in the Great Hall. If you do that, I'll put in a good word for you with Lord Cecil. He'll help you find a new situation somewhere else and you'll be able to get on with your life. Does that sound like a good plan?'

Again, he nodded.

'Good. Now I'm sure you'll be sensible and you won't give us away. But just in case you're thinking of doing anything like that, remember, the consequences for you will be *terrible*.' Alice said this in a voice as dark and cold as the Thames in winter. Her eyes bored unblinkingly into Owen's, and Tom was reminded of what an exceptionally good player she was. Her performance certainly convinced Owen, who took a deep, shuddering breath and replied: 'I'll do as you say, I promise.'

Nervously, he moved towards the door and departed. Tom picked up the now empty wine jug, which Owen had dropped during their brief fight, and resumed his position by the door. He could hear his heart thumping in his chest.

'Are you worried he'll blab to the guards?' Alice whispered.

Tom nodded, taking a firmer grip on the jug as he prepared to use it as a weapon.

'He won't,' said Alice confidently, but she, too, returned to the wall on the opposite side of the door, having armed herself with a broom.

Outside, they heard Owen addressing the guards, but could not make out his words.

This was followed by a long silence.

Finally, the guards' heavy footsteps began moving up the passageway towards the Great Hall.

Tom let out a pent-up breath. He waited for the footsteps to fade, then opened the door a crack. There was no one about. He and Alice put down their weapons and slipped out of the buttery. Tom led her on a diagonal course up the passageway and through an archway on the other side. This led to a gloomy, narrow corridor. At the far end, behind a door, lay a twisting stone staircase.

After a short ascent, they emerged in a moonlit, oak-panelled corridor adorned with paintings, a suit of armour and a large stained-glass window overlooking the courtyard. Low murmurs could be heard coming from a room across the way. Keeping to the shadowy edges of the corridor, Tom crept closer to the door of the room. Amid the low throb of voices, he recognised the earl. He sounded angry.

'Sir Gelly,' the earl was saying, 'you told me the plan was to stir up the crowd by showing them the banned scene. By all the gods, I never authorised the assassination of Lord Cecil!'

'My lord…' – this sounded like Sir Gelly – 'I recall you telling me that nothing would please you more than the death of the Beagle. You said it was your deepest wish.'

'A wish is not a command, Sir Gelly! It was never my intention to indulge in such underhand tactics. If I am to be England's next king, I must be seen to behave like one. I intend to fight for the throne in an honourable manner, not by hiring some murderous dog from the streets to kill off my rivals! What I find most exasperating of all is that your sordid little plan didn't even work. You botched it!'

'That was not our fault, my lord!' grumbled Sir Gelly. 'We planned it all meticulously. Mr Scrope has never failed us before. Somehow, that little Judas, Tom Cavendish, must have got wind of our plans. He stopped Burbage from delivering the crucial line, and then he and his player friend got to Scrope before he could kill the Beagle. If it hadn't been for them, the kingdom could have been ours by now.'

'Nevertheless, we are where we are,' came a voice Tom recognized as Lord Monteagle's. Tom exchanged a wry glance with Alice – so much for Monteagle's talk of going abroad to "lie low".

'They will undoubtedly lay siege to this house tomorrow,' said Monteagle. 'But all is not yet lost. We could make our escape tonight with a hundred men, to Wales or the English coast, and thence to Europe. Once there we will be able to regroup – raise money, arms and men for an invasion in the summer.'

This suggestion provoked angry dissent from others in the room, most especially from Sir Gelly Meyrick, who thundered: 'How, sir, can you even think of fleeing at this auspicious moment, when we have the people on our side and glory within our grasp? We should stay here and fight! Tomorrow, we should march on the palace!'

Several in the room cheered this proposal.

'The palace?' queried another voice. 'What about the Tower of London? If we seize the Tower and take possession of its armaments, our position would be immeasurably stronger.'

'We're not going to march to the Tower or the palace,' said Essex. 'Not at first anyway. We're going to march to the City. My good friend Sheriff Smyth has promised me a thousand armed militiamen. With such a force at our backs, we will be unstoppable. The public will cheer us all the way to Whitehall.'

'But my lord, our men are expecting us to march on the Palace,' pleaded Sir Gelly.

'We should go first to the Tower,' said the other voice.

'We go to the City,' insisted Essex.

Outside the room, Tom glanced at Alice. 'We should get back,' he whispered to her. 'Let Cecil know they're going to the City.'

'What if they change their minds?' asked Alice.

Tom sighed. She was right. But the longer they stayed here, the more likely it was they would get caught.

Sir Gelly was speaking again: 'My lord, the palace is just twenty minutes march from here and we have the forces to take it without need of the sheriff's men. If we march there at first light, we can take the Court by surprise. And don't forget the people. They will rally to your flag. A march into the City will waste time and hand the initiative to the Beagle.'

'Enough, Sir Gelly!' yelled Essex. 'The decision is made!'

'My lord, I cannot stand by and let you commit such folly!'

'Enough, I say!'

'Then I am done, my lord!'

This was followed by a scrape of chair legs and a burst of angry footsteps. Before Tom and Alice had time to hide, the door flew open.

Sir Gelly took one look at them and bellowed: 'Traitors!!!'

Chapter 31

The Dungeon

Tom tottered backwards in fright as Sir Gelly lunged at him. The steward grabbed him by the collar and bodily lifted him from the floor. Such was the hatred burning in Sir Gelly's eyes, Tom feared he was about to be ripped limb from limb. Meanwhile, a guard rushed out of the room and seized Alice, pinning her to the floor.

With an effort, Sir Gelly seemed to suppress his first murderous intentions and he forced Tom to his knees. He then dragged him into the room by the scruff of the neck and hurled him violently across the floor. Tom crashed painfully into a high-backed settle chair.

Dazed, he peered around the room, his mind still struggling to come to terms with this shocking turn of events. A dozen faces loomed monstrously in the candlelight, several of them familiar. As one, they looked appalled, sickened and revolted by him.

Sir Gelly unsheathed his sword. 'Let me kill the boy now, my lord,' he said, breathing hard. 'Just give me the order and I'll cleave that traitorous head from his shoulders.'

The earl took a step closer to Tom. 'Put down your sword, Sir Gelly. There will be no blood spilt in this room.'

Tom's eyes blurred with tears when he caught sight of his master. He began to sob – he couldn't help it. The earl knelt close. There was no hatred in his eyes, only pain and bewilderment, and this further compounded the hurt Tom felt.

'Why, Tom?' he murmured. 'Why this betrayal? I thought you loved me.'

'I d-did, my lord,' snivelled Tom. 'I *do!* But you have been badly... *badly* advised. It sh-should not have come to this.'

'Come to what?'

'*This!*' Tom cried, indicating the others in the room. 'S-Sir Francis was working hard on your behalf. He could have restored you to favour.'

The earl chuckled and rose to his feet. 'That ship has sailed, my friend. There is no path back to Court for me.'

'My lord, that's not true!' Tom cried. 'Tell Sir Francis that you had nothing to do with the assassination attempt. The queen will believe you!'

But Essex was no longer listening. He had turned away, and began speaking to the Earl of Southampton. 'Tell me, Henry,' he said, 'when we arrive at the Palace, where should we attack first? The Presence Chamber, or the Guard House? Do we imprison the queen, or attack the royal guards?'

'My lord!' sobbed Tom. 'Please… Aaah!' He yelled as Sir Gelly struck him hard across the face.

'Silence, traitor!' The steward turned to his master. 'My lord, shall I take him and his accomplice to the dungeon?'

'What?' Essex seemed already to have forgotten Tom. 'Oh, yes, if you would. Thank you.'

The earl's complete lack of concern was like a stab in the heart for Tom. Just moments ago, he'd seemed genuinely interested in him, even compassionate. Now it was as if Tom did not exist. This abrupt switch had to be a result of the stress he was under – it was affecting his mind.

Sir Gelly grabbed Tom's arm and began dragging him from the room. One of the guards yanked Alice to her feet. But before they reached the door, a voice spoke up from the back of the room: 'Sir Gelly, leave the prisoners to me, would you?'

The steward looked up angrily. 'This is an internal security matter, Lord Monteagle,' he snapped. 'It has nothing to do with you.'

'I can get information out of them,' said Monteagle, stepping closer. 'They must have a story to tell to explain why they are here and who sent them to snoop on us.'

'I can interrogate them myself,' said the steward.

'Yes, but you are a blunt instrument, Sir Gelly. You know how to inflict pain, but not how to exploit it to your advantage. Under your custody I guarantee that these two will be dead in under an hour and you will have nothing to show for it.'

Sir Gelly snarled at this insult.

'What makes you think you'll fare any better, William?' asked the Earl of Southampton.

Monteagle's eyes glinted dangerously. 'Let's just say I have methods… Tried and tested methods.' He approached Essex, who was studying a map of Whitehall Palace laid out upon a table in the centre of the room. 'Robert, will you release the two spies into my charge?'

'What's that?' said Essex vaguely. He glanced up. 'Oh, are they still here? Yes, take them, take them, William. Do whatever you think necessary.'

Smiling thinly through his beard, Monteagle strode over to Sir Gelly. The steward growled and reluctantly stood aside. Monteagle then instructed his two personal guards to take hold of Tom and Alice and follow him. A couple of the earl's soldiers, carrying torches, accompanied them.

Tom's captor had his upper arm in a vice-like grip as he was marched out of the room, along the upper-floor corridor and down the main stairs. He tried not to think about what was to come, but visions of whips and iron spikes kept flaring in his mind. Alice should not have been involved in any of this. If only he'd been firmer in refusing to let her come. He would tell Monteagle anything – *anything!* – to stop him hurting her.

'Take us to the dungeon,' Monteagle instructed the soldiers when they reached the lobby.

They led them into the great hall and then through a curtained arch near the enormous hearth. This led to a set of stone steps that twisted downwards into darkness. The soldiers led the way, and the flickering light from their torches played ominously on the ancient brickwork. The man holding Tom tightened his grip as they descended, in case he tried to break free, and Tom's arm began to feel numb. At the bottom of the steps one of the soldiers used a key on his belt to open an iron-studded door, and Tom and Alice were shoved into the dungeon. Tom shivered in the cold, damp, subterranean air. The soldiers lit the wall-torches, illuminating a bleak, dismal place with low arched ceilings and black stone walls that had chains bolted to them for securing prisoners. Tom was relieved to note the absence of any hideous torture contraptions. Still, there was no end of suffering that could be inflicted with fire and fists, and Monteagle's guards had arms packed with muscles.

The one holding Tom took a torch from one of the soldiers and held it close to Tom's face, causing him to recoil from the intense heat and light.

'You were sent by Lord Cecil, am I right, boy?' asked Monteagle.

There was no point in resisting. 'Aye,' Tom croaked.

'Good.'

Monteagle then nodded to his guards. They immediately released Tom and Alice and threw themselves at the earl's soldiers, their fists flying. Within seconds, both soldiers were on the floor, unconscious.

Tom stared in shock at the fallen men and then at their assailants.

'What's going on?' he heard Alice ask.

They turned back to Monteagle, searching for an explanation.

Monteagle was holding a scroll, which he handed to Tom. 'I'm setting you free,' he told them both, 'because I want you to pass this to Lord Cecil. It lays out my terms for giving evidence against the Earl of Essex at his trial once this rebellion is crushed – for it will be crushed. Those men upstairs are deluded if they believe otherwise. I wish they'd heeded my advice – we could have all been on our way to the nearest border by now. Instead, they seem obsessed with honour and glory, even if that means death. More's the pity, for of all the rebellions I have been involved in, this one had the best chance of success. The queen is old and weak – Essex is genuinely popular with the masses. It's a shame he's such a fool. Still, I don't intend to go down with him. That letter represents my escape route from the executioner's axe. Be sure it gets to Lord Cecil.'

Hardly daring to believe their luck, Tom and Alice followed Monteagle and his guards out of the dungeon and back up the stairs into the great hall. In the lobby, Monteagle bade them farewell, explaining that he had to return to the meeting upstairs.

'If anyone asks, I will tell them that my men are still working on you,' he said with a smile. 'They probably won't ask – those men have larger matters on their minds right now.'

Tom couldn't help thinking that this was all some cruel game on the part of Monteagle, designed to give them hope before he snatched them back. After all, he'd played a similar trick on Gus Phillips. But as they followed the guards into the garden and along the path that led towards the river, fear began to shade into hope. He and Alice kept their heads down as Monteagle's men flashed their insignia and gave orders to the guards to open the watergate. There was no trouble. Monteagle was a trusted friend of the earl's. On the jetty, Tom used one of the guard's torches to signal to their barge, which soon appeared through the mist. And just a quarter of an hour after they had been led as prisoners into a dungeon in fear of their lives, Tom and Alice found themselves heading back to the palace.

Chapter 32

The Rebellion

At half past ten the following morning, the Earl of Essex rode out of Essex House at the head of some two hundred men. 'To the palace!' the soldiers cried, and they were confused when the earl instead turned east towards the City. The men began to mutter among themselves: surely their enemies lay to the west in Whitehall Palace? No one had bothered to explain to them the earl's strategy of marching first to the City to link up with the reinforcements promised by Sheriff Smyth.

The rebel army progressed down the Strand, along Fleet Street and then through the Lud Gate in the City wall. As they climbed Lud Gate Hill, Essex cried out for support from the locals. Perhaps he was thinking of the scene at the end of Shakespeare's *Richard II,* in which Henry of Bolingbroke was cheered through the City. It was his favourite scene in the play. But real life did not work out that way for Essex. The locals who turned out did not cheer him. They simply stared as he and his followers went by. No one joined their ranks.

'We march for England!' proclaimed Essex. 'We march to save this country from the evil Lord Cecil, who wants to sell us to the Spanish!' He had heard rumours that the Beagle was negotiating for the King of Spain's daughter to succeed Elizabeth. Whether true or not, he had hoped it would prove a popular rallying cry. A few citizens booed politely, but they did not join the march.

At the top of Lud Gate Hill, Essex hoped to catch the crowds who had gathered for the mid-morning sermon at St Paul's Cross, but he was too late – the congregation had dispersed. Surprised and disappointed that London was not flocking to his banner, the earl rode down Cheapside, Poultry Street and Lombard Street, heading towards Fenchurch Street and the home of Sheriff Smyth. Here, surely, he would be guaranteed a warm welcome!

He arrived just in time to catch Smyth slipping out of the back door. The sheriff had no men, and denied ever having promised any. Essex was crushed. 'What do you mean?' he remonstrated. 'You gave me your word!'

'The Beagle is behind this,' Sir Gelly insisted. 'He

must have threatened the sheriff!'

'But how did Cecil find out about our plans?' Essex wanted to know. 'We only decided on this course of action last night!'

More bad news soon followed: a scout reported that the Earl of Cumberland had been seen leading a detachment of troops towards the City, and a chain had been drawn across the Lud Gate. Essex and his men were trapped!

'It's almost as if the Beagle knew what we were up to!' the earl lamented. 'He let us come into the City, and now he's sealed us off from our base, and from the palace. But how did he learn of our intentions?'

'Spies!' Sir Gelly muttered darkly. 'Traitors in our midst!'

The earl's reaction surprised him, for he suddenly declared: 'We need food!'

And so the rebellion broke off for lunch.

With the sheriff gone, the rebels commandeered his house as a base, raiding his kitchens for food and ale. As they ate, they could hear heralds in the street proclaiming Essex a traitor and promising a royal pardon for those who were prepared to desert him. The earl laughed this off – 'a herald will proclaim anything for a couple of shillings!' – but he could not avoid noticing that his followers were shrinking in number. Many had taken the opportunity to slink away during luncheon, including Lord Cromwell and the Earls of Sussex and Bedford.

Realising at last that his situation had grown perilous, the earl abandoned his meal and, with his napkin still around his neck, charged out into the street to rally his remaining troops. He decided his best hope lay in a return to Essex House, so he led his dwindling band of followers back towards the Lud Gate. On the way, they were met again by Sheriff Smyth, who begged Essex to surrender to the authorities. The earl ignored him and rode on. The rebels were checked at the Lud Gate by the chain drawn across it and by a line of pikemen under the command of the Earl of Cumberland.

There followed an uncomfortable stand-off between the two sides, which lasted until a hot-headed rebel discharged his pistol into the pikemen. The defensive line failed to buckle, however, so Essex called upon his men to charge. Only one did, and he was badly injured in the cheek. Now it was the pikemen's turn to charge, whereupon Essex turned and fled with his followers back up Lud Gate Hill. By now a truly sorry and bedraggled bunch, they tried to escape down Friday Street to the river. This street, they discovered, had also been blocked off, but compassionate citizens raised the chain to let them through to the Thames. Several nearly drowned in the scramble for boats. Eventually, they made it onto the river and thence back to Essex House.

The earl was in a state of nervous exhaustion by this time. Dazed and sweating and no longer capable of leadership, he retired to his private quarters. As dusk fell, royalist forces began to converge on Essex House, positioning themselves along the Strand and even occupying its gardens, cutting off any hope of escape by river. Forces under the command of Lord Burghley broke into the courtyard and began firing at the windows, shattering the earl's collection of Venetian glassware and blowing holes in several of his Flemish tapestries.

At just after ten o'clock that night, the Earl of Essex and his remaining supporters and followers emerged from Essex House into a torchlit courtyard to be taken into custody. They were conveyed by river to Lambeth Palace and from there by horse and carriage to the Tower of London. The Essex Rebellion was over. It had lasted just twelve hours.

Epilogue

9th February 1601

'Thank you, my young friends,' Lord Cecil said to Tom and Alice the following morning. 'Your information about the rebels' plans proved invaluable. They allowed me to ensnare Essex first in the City and then, after his escape from there, in his own home.'

The three of them were walking along one of the many corridors in the confusing labyrinth of Whitehall Palace.

'What will happen to him?' asked Tom, feeling a tug of pity for his former master.

'There will be a trial,' said Cecil. 'He will be found guilty of treason, of course, and then he will be executed.'

'And Sir Gelly?'

'Yes, him too.'

'And Lord Monteagle will, I suppose, be set free?' asked Alice.

Cecil grimaced at the mention of the man's name. 'Yes, that wily old snake has done enough to ensure his survival once again. I really thought I had him this time – but no! He offered a deal that I could not refuse. The trouble is he knows too much – both about the Essex plot and others currently being hatched against us in Europe. In short, he has proved himself too valuable to be killed. So I must, as usual, set aside my personal loathing of the man for the good of the nation. He will be fined, of course, and then he will be set free once more to wreak mischief in that grey world he inhabits between lawfulness and treachery.'

'Sire, there is one other matter that still concerns me,' ventured Alice.

'And what is that?' asked Cecil.

'My brother, Richard, has been missing for more than a week. He was used by Edmund Squires to deliver a message to the assassin, Mr Scrope. Almost certainly, Mr Scrope killed him after receiving the message. I am prepared to accept this, yet I cannot rest easy until I know for sure that Richard is dead. I am haunted by the possibility that he may still be alive somewhere in need of my help. Perhaps Edmund knows something. Mr Scrope may have told him of Richard's fate…'

Lord Cecil had started shaking his head long before she had finished speaking. 'We have questioned

Squires extensively about the plot,' he told her. 'He has proved very obliging in all respects, but swears he does not know what became of your brother. All he would say on the matter was this: Mr Scrope was instructed to kill Richard and Mr Scrope was always very reliable when it came to carrying out orders... I'm afraid, Adam, that you may never obtain physical proof of your brother's death, but you will have to try and accept it nonetheless.'

Alice bit her lip and blinked away some tears, and Tom could see that Cecil was asking far too much of her in this regard.

They turned a corner and came upon a man standing by himself gazing up at a painting on the wall. He was short with reddish brown hair and a neat, pointed beard.

'Sir Francis!' cried Tom, forgetting all decorum in his excitement at encountering him.

Sir Francis Bacon turned and greeted him with a warm smile. 'Well met, young Tom,' he said. 'And you, too, Adam Fletcher. It is an honour to meet the pair who managed to crack the assassin's code.'

He beckoned to them and they gathered before the painting he had been studying. It was a portrait of a king. He was dressed in an ermine robe with a jewelled collar to match his jewelled crown. His face, Tom thought, was innocent and somewhat anxious, like that of a nervous child.

'Who is it?' asked Alice.

'Richard II,' answered Cecil. 'Not like our queen at

all, is he?'

'A decent enough man, I'm sure,' remarked Sir Francis, 'but not really cut out for kingship. Unlike this one...' He pointed to the portrait next to it.

The man in this painting had a strong face, a long dark beard, a furrowed brow and dark eyes that seemed to radiate an iron will. He looked, in Tom's view, every inch a king.

'That's King Henry IV,' said Cecil. 'Or, as I like to think of him, the usurper Henry of Bolingbroke.'

'Whatever you wish to call him, he was a born leader,' commented Sir Francis. 'And this was the reason why the Essex Rebellion was always doomed to fail. In terms of leadership, Essex was far worse than Bolingbroke, and Elizabeth is far better than Richard.'

'Are you saying the rebellion would have failed with or without us?' asked Alice.

'Yes, I am,' nodded Sir Francis, 'but your actions prevented it from becoming a prolonged and bloody affair that would have left a lasting scar on our country, and for that we owe you our thanks.'

A servant arrived dressed with almost absurd elegance in velvet, silk and cloth of gold. 'The queen is ready to receive you in the Presence Chamber,' he announced.

Tom gulped. He felt the touch of Alice's hand on his arm, and looked across to see her smiling at him. Of course, she'd been through all this before. As the servant went through the protocol, Alice mouthed the words, imitating the servant's supercilious expression

– 'Do not speak unless spoken to… Do not approach her majesty, but always remain at least six paces from her person…' Tom found it hard not to giggle at Alice's performance. At one point, he audibly sniggered, provoking sharp frowns from both the servant and Lord Cecil.

At length, the servant finished his monologue. Guards threw open the doors, and they were ushered into the Presence Chamber. It was a huge room with a shiny marble floor and gilded walls hung with tapestries. Queen Elizabeth was seated on a small dais surrounded by her ladies in waiting. She wore a white gown embroidered with gold thread and encrusted with dozens of glittering jewels. Her head was framed by an extravagant ruff. She held a fan that, from time to time, she fluttered before her face.

Alice had warned Tom that she looked a lot older than her portraits, yet on first sighting he saw only a dazzling beauty. Pale gold light streamed in from windows high above, shining upon her auburn hair, pale skin and red lips. It was as he drew closer that he began to see the ravages of age – the gauntness and the wrinkles. He saw, too, what no amount of make-up could conceal, which was the redness around her eyes – the queen had been crying.

They all bowed deeply as Sir Francis made the introductions. The queen expressed delight at seeing young Adam again, and gratitude to both he and Tom for their brave actions in defence of her realm.

'I vowed to myself yesternight that I would not retire to my bed until the Earl of Essex was safely under lock and key,' she confided to them. 'The news was told to me at three o'clock, and off to bed I went. But I did not sleep even then. I wept all night. I know not why.'

'She loves him, doesn't she?' remarked Alice.

Sir Francis smiled sadly at this, his eyes far away. 'In her own way, she does,' he said. 'But she's always been a monarch first and a woman second. She may be weeping now, but it won't stop her from signing his death warrant when the time comes...'

After they had departed the palace, Sir Francis invited Tom and Alice back to his house for some luncheon. They had eagerly accepted the invitation and here they were now, seated in Sir Francis's luxurious barge, heading east along the Thames towards York House. There was a crisp, raw breeze bearing icy droplets of rain, and the river was the colour of cold steel. Yet it was cosy beneath the barge's canopy, and Tom was immoderately happy in the company of his two favourite people.

'I remember a time long ago,' said Sir Francis, 'when the Earl of Essex first got into trouble over something or other. Back then, people would talk about how he divided the court – how he had his friends and his enemies. Well, I told them back then and I will tell you now, Essex has always had just one friend and one enemy, and that friend is the queen, and that enemy is himself.'

Tom was surprised to see a tear in Sir Francis's eye. He wiped it away, a little abashed that Tom had seen it. 'It is cold,' he said, hugging himself.

'No one could have done more than you, sir, to reconcile them,' said Tom. 'You tried until the very end.'

Sir Francis smiled and nodded, seemingly comforted by this. 'And what will *you* do, Tom,' he asked, 'now that you have lost your master?'

'I shall seek a position in another household, sir.'

'Might you possibly be interested in a position at York House?'

Tom stared at him. His mouth opened, but no words emerged. He could not imagine anything he wanted more.

'Take a few days to think about it,' offered Sir Francis.

'Nay, sir,' cried Tom, 'I do not need any time to think about it. I would be delighted to accept your offer. Thank you, sir. With all my heart, thank you!'

'You're very welcome,' laughed Sir Francis. 'You may start immediately, if you like. I have need of a groom, you see, owing to the recent departure of my young man, Nicholas. After luncheon, you can return to Essex House to retrieve your possessions. There will be a room for you in the roof…'

Alice listened to the two of them eagerly making arrangements for Tom's employment at York House. She was happy for Tom, for she knew how much he liked and admired Sir Francis. Yet she also felt a twinge of sadness, having dared hope that her new friend might wish to join her at the Globe. Perhaps the life of a player was not for him though, despite his habit of making frequent, if unplanned, appearances on the stage!

As for herself, the future seemed like a bleak and unfriendly place without her brother. Edmund's betrayal was another bitter blow. Yet, if she had proved anything to herself in these past few days it was that she was a survivor. More than that, she was a fighter, who had helped foil a dangerous rebellion. Also, she had met Tom, who seemed to her like a true and loyal friend. Now that she thought about it, perhaps the future wasn't quite so bleak after all!

Sneak preview of
The Shakespeare Plot
Book 2

The Dark Forest

Chapter 1

The Rescue

Warwickshire, 24th March 1603

The young man moved silently through the forest. His feet padded softly upon the earth, negotiating the knotty roots of the ancient oak trees with the stealth of a wolf. An arrow lay against the notch of his handmade bow, ready to be fired. His hopeful, fearful eyes were ever on the alert for movement – be it caused by predator or prey. His clothes were no more than rags, his skin rough and dark.

Yesterday he had spent in similar fashion, and also the day before that. This was his life – forever on the move, never sleeping in the same place for more than one night. His only possessions were his bow and arrow, and his knife. Once, he supposed, he may have had a patch of earth where he belonged, somewhere he could call home. If so, he did not remember it. For countless moons, he had lived this way – a drifter, spurred onwards by the hope of finding food and by the fear of being found by the Evil One who was never far behind him.

He was lonely, though he did not know it – for all he had ever been, at least in his memory, was alone. What most would call loneliness, he only felt as a melancholy emptiness at his core, a sense that there must be more to life than this endless cycle of hunger, thirst, fear and exhaustion.

In the afternoon, he chanced upon a babbling brook and he fell to the ground and drank greedily from it, not realising until that moment how parched he was. Shortly afterwards, he killed a squirrel for his evening meal, which he then tied by its tail to his belt. As the shafts of light through the forest canopy turned a reddish gold, he began to search for a place to rest his head for the night. As usual, he desired a spot easily camouflaged with branches and forest litter, but which also offered him a vantage point to watch for the Evil One. At length, he found a suitable spot beneath an enormous tree root growing out of the bank of a dried-up stream bed. He set about finding leafy branches to disguise and give added shelter to his new home. Once satisfied with his little den, the young man set about collecting firewood.

Dusk had fallen by the time he could rest his limbs

by the crackling fire. He gutted the squirrel with his knife, skewered it with a sharpened stick, then began to turn it above the flames on a makeshift spit made from two forked branches. Even now, he did not relax his vigil on the trees, and his bow and arrow was always within easy reach.

As he lay upon his bed in the darkness, listening to the soft music of the crickets, frogs and night birds, he asked himself the same questions that tormented him every night. *Does the Evil One really exist? Why does it never show itself?* At times like these, the temptation arose simply to stay put – to make his latest shelter his home. But even in these moments he knew, in his heart, that he would never stop moving. For he was sure the Evil One *did* exist – whether it was truly evil or not the young man could not say – but it was always there. Sometimes, as he walked through the forest, he felt its presence close behind. Occasionally he might hear a rustle of leaves or the snap of a twig to his rear, but saw no animal nor any possible cause for the sound when he turned to look. Now and then he would hear a whisper, like the wind through branches, on a windless day. Once or twice he even fancied he felt the touch of a warm breath upon his neck. At such times, he would always quicken his pace, and with nervous fingers he'd place an arrow at the ready in his bow – but he would not dare turn to see who or what was there.

The next morning, the young man rose before sunrise, destroyed his shelter and kicked over the ashes of his fire, removing all traces of his presence. With a fearful glance over his shoulder – for he sensed the Evil One close on his heels – he struck out into the forest, following an animal trail that he hoped might lead to a source of water and perhaps some breakfast.

The sun was about a quarter of the way through its arc and the young man was starting to feel the familiar pangs of hunger and thirst when he suddenly stopped and became extremely still. An unusual and frightening sound was coming through the trees from the north. It was the sound of human voices. The young man was not unacquainted with his own kind. From time to time, he had met and spoken to fellow wanderers in the forest. But those humans he had encountered had always been softly spoken – forest dwellers like himself. The voices he could hear now were sharp as thorns, and bitter as unripe berries. He sensed violence in their tone and it scared him. Keeping low to the ground, he crept closer to the source of the voices until he found himself on the edge of a clearing.

In its midst he spied four men on horseback. Three of them wore hooded cloaks and masks over their faces. They were threatening the fourth man with swords and pistols. The fourth man seemed angry rather than intimidated. He had a florid face, a full beard and long hair, and was shouting at them to put down their weapons and let him pass. The men showed no signs of doing so. All he succeeded in doing was to make them angry, and soon enough one of them trotted up and struck the bearded man hard on the side of the head with the flat of his sword. This caused him to topple off his horse and crash to the ground.

The young man, watching from behind a tree, flinched at the sight of this brutal act. He stared, appalled, as the attacker and his friends dismounted and surrounded the fallen figure, pointing their weapons at him. 'Hand over your money, wretch, and we might just let you live!' said one of them.

The young man was, by nature, cautious, and his first instinct was to flee. And yet he felt sympathy for this brave man, and disgust at the savage treatment he was suffering at the hands of these bandits. He wanted to intervene, but remained hesitant. Why risk his own life by helping a stranger?

It was when the bandits began to kick their victim, hard, in the legs and torso, that the young man made up his mind. In one swift movement, he pulled an arrow from his quiver, drew his bow and fired...

The arrow flew through the air and struck one of the bandits in the leg. He screamed and fell over. The other two bandits spun around to see where the arrow had come from. As they did so, another arrow shot out of the trees and pierced the hat of one of them. Then a third arrow whistled through the sleeve of the other one's jerkin, narrowly missing his arm. This was all too much for the bandits. They turned and leapt upon their horses, before galloping away into the forest, leaving their wounded comrade still writhing around on the ground.

With the danger now gone, the young man emerged from his hiding-place. He ran to where the wounded bandit lay and removed the sword from his hand, in case he tried to attack him. Then he helped the other man to his feet.

'God grant you mercy, kind sir!' the man said hoarsely. 'That was quite exceptional shooting. I owe you my life.'

Unused to speech and somewhat embarrassed by this display of gratitude, the young man merely nodded.

'Is there anything I can do to repay you?'

The young man pointed to the water bottle attached to the saddle of the other man's horse.

'Why of course! Please drink!'

He handed him the bottle. After taking a deep and much needed swig, the young man handed it back, then turned and began to walk away.

'Prithee, do not go so soon,' said the man. 'Tell me who you are, at least, and how you come to be in these parts. Or am I to think you some guardian spirit of the forest sent here to protect unwary travellers? Tell me, are you flesh and blood?'

The young man paused in his stride and frowned at this strange question.

'Whatever you are,' the man continued, 'I would welcome your companionship, not to mention your protection, for the remainder of my journey. I live not far from here, at a place called Baddesley Clinton... But where are my manners? I should have introduced myself.' He gave a bow. 'I am Griffin Markham, a soldier. And to whom do I owe the pleasure…?'

The young man did not reply. He was thinking: *What should I do? Should I go with him? I know nothing of this fellow. He may imprison or enslave me. On the other hand, he seems kind enough. Perhaps he will offer me food and shelter at this Baddesley Clinton – and protection from the Evil One.*

He was interrupted in these thoughts by a groan from the wounded bandit. Glancing down, he saw the man had managed to pull the arrow from his leg, and had then fainted from the pain. The arrowhead was slick with dark blood. The wound, however, was not too deep. It would heal if cared for.

Eventually, the young man came to a decision. He looked again at Griffin Markham. 'I will go with you…' he said. The words sounded strange in his ears. His tongue felt thick and clumsy. It had been so long since he'd spoken.

Markham clapped his hands in delight. 'You speak! How splendid! And of your decision, I heartily approve!'

'We must take this man, too,' said the young man. 'He will die if we leave him here.'

'A fitting end for a no-good footpad such as he, wouldn't you say?' responded Markham as he remounted his horse. 'Come, let's leave him for the wolves. You can take his horse.'

The young man did not move, and Markham was forced to relent. 'Very well,' he sighed. 'We'll take him with us. There is a physician in the village who can tend to his leg.'

After heaving the unconscious bandit onto the back of his horse, the young man climbed into the saddle. He had no memory of riding, and yet he found that his hands and legs knew what to do. Soon, he and Markham were riding side by side along the forest trail.

'You don't speak much,' commented Markham as they rode.

The young man glanced to the rear.

'And why do you keep doing that?' said Markham. 'You keep looking behind you. Are you being followed?'

Impatient at his companion's continued silence, Markham said at last: 'I must confess to an uncommon curiosity about you, young stranger. Pray tell me your story. From where do you hail?'

'I know not,' answered the young man truthfully. 'For as long as I can remember, I have been roaming these woods.'

'That is quite extraordinary!' declared Markham. 'Forsooth, perhaps I was right after all to call you a spirit of the forest. Do you recall nothing at all of your early life?'

'I remember once I had a name,' said the young man, after a short pause.

'And what was it?'

'People used to call me… Richard Fletcher.'

TO BE CONTINUED...

A selected list of Scribo titles

The prices shown below are correct at the time of going to press. However, The Salariya Book Company reserves the right to show new retail prices on covers, which may differ from those previously advertised.

Gladiator School by Dan Scott

1 Blood Oath	978-1-908177-48-3	£6.99
2 Blood & Fire	978-1-908973-60-3	£6.99
3 Blood & Sand	978-1-909645-16-5	£6.99
4 Blood Vengeance	978-1-909645-62-2	£6.99
5 Blood & Thunder	978-1-910184-20-2	£6.99
6 Blood Justice	978-1-910184-43-1	£6.99

Iron Sky by Alex Woolf

1 Dread Eagle	978-1-909645-00-4	£9.99
2 Call of the Phoenix	978-1-910184-87-5	£6.99

Aldo Moon by Alex Woolf

1 Aldo Moon and the Ghost at Gravewood Hall	978-1-908177-84-1	£6.99

Chronosphere by Alex Woolf

1 Time out of Time	978-1-907184-55-0	£6.99
2 Malfunction	978-1-907184-56-7	£6.99
3 Ex Tempora	978-1-908177-87-2	£6.99